"I'm here for you, Charly. Tell me how to help."

"Who the hell *are* you?"

"It's me, Will Chase. Were you expecting someone else?"

Yeah, she was expecting one of the bad guys. She still expected one or all of them to burst out of the night and attack. "You're working for them."

"Absolutely not. I'm on your side. You have to believe that."

She did. On instinct, she did believe him. Though she didn't understand how it was possible for him to be here.

"Charly, sit down here beside me."

"We're not safe here."

"Sure we are."

She shook her head, wobbling a bit. Shivering, she didn't protest when he put her back into her polar-fleece coat and wrapped an arm around her waist. She felt the weight of her revolver in her pocket. If he was with the bad guys, he wouldn't let her keep her weapons. He guided her under the shelter of an overhang and helped her sit down.

Her body recognized him even if her mind argued obstinately. Relaxing into his embrace, she let her head drop to his shoulder.

HEART OF A HERO

USA TODAY Bestselling Authors

DEBRA WEBB
& REGAN BLACK

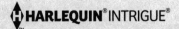

From Regan: To Jordan, for being my brilliant, beautiful star. Your wisdom and compassion are as wide as the sky and your future as limitless.

ISBN-13: 978-0-373-74867-9

Heart of a Hero

Copyright © 2015 by Debra Webb

Recycling programs for this product may not exist in your area.

Printed in U.S.A.

www.Harlequin.com

Debra Webb, born in Alabama, wrote her first story at age nine and her first romance at thirteen. It wasn't until she spent three years working for the military behind the Iron Curtain—and a five-year stint with NASA—that she realized her true calling. Since then the *USA TODAY* bestselling author has penned more than one hundred novels, including her internationally bestselling Colby Agency series.

Regan Black, a *USA TODAY* bestselling author, writes award-winning, action-packed novels featuring kick-butt heroines and the sexy heroes who fall in love with them. Raised in the Midwest and California, she and her family, along with their adopted greyhound, two arrogant cats and a quirky finch, reside in the South Carolina Lowcountry, where the rich blend of legend, romance and history fuels her imagination.

CAST OF CHARACTERS

Charlotte (Charly) Binali—Charly is a sixth-generation wilderness guide in Durango, Colorado, considered part bloodhound by her peers and local law enforcement officials.

William Chase—A former navy SEAL, Will is now assigned to Colorado as part of director Casey's elite deep-cover task force.

Thomas Casey—The director of the Specialists has one last task force to assemble as he nears retirement.

Reed Lancaster—Has spent his career overcoming a disastrous setback when his software innovations were stolen. Now he has his revenge in sight.

Chapter One

"I'm in. But I'm not wearing the shorts."

Director Thomas Casey eyed William Chase, one of the newest recruits to his team known as the Specialists. He respected independent thinkers. Went out of his way to select highly skilled individuals who knew how to solve problems quickly and creatively. Still, it was rare when anyone on his handpicked team showed this kind of attitude. Maybe he'd made a mistake with this cocky young guy fresh from an elite Navy SEAL team.

"A uniform is a uniform," Thomas said, keeping his voice even.

"That's true, sir," Will agreed. "And it should convey authority."

Thomas couldn't believe he was having this discussion with so many bigger issues at play.

"You'll have time to come to terms with how the US Postal Service conveys authority in Colorado before the weather warms up out there." He wanted someone on his new task force planted in the middle of the country. Someone who could respond effectively to a variety of situations.

"Shorts are for kids and physical training. Are you going to pull me off this operation if I don't wear the shorts?"

Thomas reached out and closed the plain manila file outlining Will's assignment. *Potential assignment.* It could've been worse, Thomas supposed. He could be having this conversation in a public setting rather than the absolute privacy of his office. He couldn't get a read on whether or not Will was kidding around. The uncertainty and unease set off warning bells in his head. He considered asking why the shorts were such a big deal and decided it didn't matter. Through the years, he'd worked with so many men and women, those who did the impossible tasks in the field and those who worked right here supporting them. Eventually his luck with recruiting was bound to run out. One more sign that it was time to retire and put his personal life, his hopes for a family, ahead of the nation's problems. But his nation needed him, had demanded his expertise one last time. If he assembled the right team, he could walk away with confidence.

"I've changed my mind, Will. You're not the right man for this job after all."

"Because I won't deliver mail in those ridiculous shorts?"

Thomas drummed his fingers on the file, met Will's stony gaze. This recruit might be a bit too independent. "Because you're agitated over a small conformity issue and that makes me question what you'll do when the stakes are higher."

"Agitated is a bit of a stretch." The smile on Will's face didn't reach his serious eyes. "You have to agree every postman who complies with that dress code is nothing more than a sheep."

"Thank you for your time," Thomas said, determined to go with a different Specialist for this post.

Will didn't budge. "Forget the shorts. Forget agitated. You saw this one—" he pointed to the folder "—whatever it is, and chose me because I succeed, *always*, when the stakes are highest."

"I was wrong," Thomas said with a casual hitch of his shoulders. "It happens. Close the door on your way out."

"No, sir. I want this assignment."

Thomas laughed. Couldn't stop it. *No one* gave him this much trouble, other than his wife, and that had been long before they married. He shouldn't find it refreshing. "You think you know how far you can push me?"

"No, sir. I know how far I can push myself."

"From my perspective you can't push yourself far enough to comply with the basic standards of your operation."

"The shorts are irrelevant, in any circumstance. You need someone willing to dig in for the long haul. Colorado was built by rugged individuals who don't see conformity as strength. They value independence and wide-open spaces and they respect people with conviction."

"So this conversation was your attempt at an audition?" Thomas wasn't laughing now. "That's not how we do things here."

"It's how they do things there." Will's eyes, intent and serious, underscored his point.

Thomas turned to his computer monitor and adjusted his glasses, going over Will's service record one more time. "Tell me what happened at Christmas."

Will didn't evade or protest, didn't get defensive or make excuses. No sign of agitation or argument now. Easing back into the chair, he smoothed his relaxed hands over his thighs. "Not much typically happens in the way of celebrating Christmas in Afghanistan unless you're on a military installation."

Thomas still had the formal report up on his

computer; he'd reviewed it one last time before Will had walked into the office. Officially, Will had been in the nosebleed section of the mountains tracking down a terrorist cell that had gone inactive due to the harsh winter weather.

"And I wasn't on base over the holiday."

"You didn't have a chance to go home?" Thomas was impressed with the way Will maintained his composure. Maybe this was the real man, the real professional he'd been looking for since the meeting began.

"Didn't take it," Will replied with a dismissive twitch of his shoulders. "The other guys had family missing them. My parents were doing fine."

"I'm sure they missed you."

Will leaned forward. "If you're worried I'll crack or break cover, that's not a problem," he said. "I've been away from home a long time, sir. The scarcity works for my family."

"All right." Thomas rolled his hand. "Go on."

"As you know, recon and surveillance is long, quiet work, and I'm good at it. You get a sense of people when you're watching them day and night."

Thomas agreed, glancing away from the computer and giving Will another long study. Everything but today's meeting told him this was the right man for the Colorado job. Maybe the former SEAL was dealing with a postdeployment conflict with authority or some personality clash. But this new task force was too important. Thomas had to be sure Will could handle the emotional pressure of deep undercover work as well as the physical strain.

"I'd been keeping an eye on the family for days. The middle daughter hauled water every day. I knew her routine. The target had been spotted to the south and then I went days with no sign of him. On December 25, I noticed the water girl's routine changed. She made one extra trip, using a different footpath."

"You followed her."

"Right to the target, yes, sir." Will dipped his chin. Eyes calm and steady. "I made the report. It felt like the perfect gift at the time."

Thomas waited, but Will didn't seem inclined to share the rest of the story. "It took you two days to get your target out of that cave and into custody."

Will dipped his chin. "That's what the report says."

Thomas leaned forward. "Do you want the post in Colorado?"

"Yes, sir. Delivering mail and chatting up locals beats the hell out of crawling through caves on the other side of the world."

"Then tell me what really happened."

"I suppose you have the clearance," Will said on a heavy sigh.

Thomas managed to stifle his laughter this time.

"I refused to move in immediately," Will began. "On the twenty-fifth."

"You didn't want to make an arrest on Christmas Day?" Thomas asked, pushing harder than he wanted to. This interview was like pulling teeth.

"Everyone acts like I was sitting around waiting for Santa Claus," Will snapped, lurching up and out of the chair. "I didn't want the water girl to *die* on Christmas. Is that so damned terrible?" He stalked over to the window, hands braced on his hips. "If I'd gone in right after her they would've known. If somehow I couldn't take them all, if I missed just *one* man, she would've been killed for sure. I have enough blood on my hands."

He turned away, but Thomas didn't need the eye contact to know Will was thinking of his brother. The Chase family had buried their younger son after a training accident. Somehow, the grief had twisted, and Will carried guilt and blame because his brother had been inspired by Will's military service.

"So, yes," Will continued, turning back. "I waited. I came at them from a different direction. I practically laid a trail for them to find me in the secondary post."

"But they didn't."

"No." His wide shoulders rolled back. "And I took them all, starting with the weakest link in their watch rotation, until it was just a matter of escorting the target to the extraction point."

Thomas knew the target remained in custody, the terrorist cell out of commission, the attack they'd planned for spring thwarted. "You saved her."

"Hard to say." Will pressed his lips together. He walked behind the chair, his fingers digging into the upholstery. "She didn't die on Christmas because of me. That's all I know for sure."

Here were the character and integrity Thomas had sensed when evaluating Will as a potential recruit. Internal fortitude and an undefinable X factor that couldn't always be measured by personnel records and reports were essential for this new task force. He nodded, calmer now that his instincts had finally been confirmed. "Pick up your travel documents and postal service new-hire information from my receptionist. What you make of the rest of your new life out there is up to you."

Will's face brightened with enthusiasm. "Thank you, sir."

"Despite your cover, you'll find a way to stay

in contact with this office and stay in combat shape. There's no way to tell when we'll call you into action."

"You won't be sorry."

Thomas leaned back into his chair after Will walked out, more than a little relieved. If the current rumors could be trusted, they might be calling on Will sooner than anyone expected.

Chapter Two

Durango, Colorado
Tuesday, February 24, 2:15 p.m.

Charlotte Binali, Charly to everyone who knew her, muttered encouragement to her computer screen. The spreadsheet was almost complete, and she didn't want to offend the technology gremlins by looking away at a crucial moment.

Her coworkers teased her mercilessly about her tenuous relationship with technology. Give her a mountain and a footprint and she could hike any terrain to find anything or anyone, but computers and the entire mess inside them made her want to cry like a baby.

She really needed to hand more of the tech over to someone else on staff, but Binali Backcountry was hers now, and as the sixth generation, she was determined to bring the business into the twenty-first century.

"Charly?" Tammy, the newest employee,

whom Charly had hired to greet customers and maintain the storefront, leaned into the office doorway. "Better break out the lip gloss. Your boyfriend's almost here."

Charly refused to take the bait, determined to finish the spreadsheet. Besides, her requisite lip balm had protective sunscreen, not shine.

"Lip gloss, stat!" Tammy urged before she disappeared from view.

The door chimed, and when Charly heard the smooth rumble of his voice, it was more of a challenge to keep herself on task. Just a few more clicks and she could give in to the distraction of the new mailman.

Tammy reappeared, a dazzled smile on her face. "He wants to know if you have a minute," she said in a whisper loud enough to be heard for miles.

Charly saved the changes to the schedule and pushed back from the desk. "Thanks," she replied, mimicking Tammy's loud whisper as she left the office to greet Will Chase, the hot new mail carrier working Durango's business district.

Hot *is a significant understatement*, she thought when he smiled at her. The strong, square jaw might have been carved from granite, and the wide shoulders, trim hips and strong hands had been starring in her dreams recently. Not that she'd admit that to anyone.

"Hey, Will."

"Hi," he replied, removing his sunglasses. "Am I interrupting?"

"No." She hoped her smile didn't look as star-struck as Tammy's. "Just finished." They'd only been out on two occasions—she couldn't bring herself to call them dates—but she melted a little every time he looked at her with those vivid eyes as deep and blue as a high mountain lake. It still startled her the way he could turn the pale, watered-down blue of the official postal service shirt and dark jeans into raw sex appeal. "Excel didn't implode on me this time."

"Glad to hear it."

Last week, when she'd been ready to smash the computer to bits one afternoon, he'd arrived with the mail, caught her midrant and given her a quick lesson on the program. Later, during what should have been movie night, he'd spent hours showing her where to find more video tutorials, which had saved her computer from going out the window more than once in the days since.

"Are we still on for a movie tonight?"

"Sure." She accepted the stack of mail, thick with outdoor-gear catalogs. "The schedule's set for next week and this time it doesn't even need to be labeled as 'The Spreadsheet that Conquered Charly.'"

He laughed, the sound as clear and fresh to her ears as a brimming creek on a hot day. "That might be the one title I don't have. I've got plenty of beer. You bring the pizza." He put his sunglasses in place and backed toward the door, graceful as a cat. "Say, seven?"

She nodded, her mouth going dry as he turned to make his exit.

Beside her, Tammy sighed. The girl liked nothing better than a clear view of an excellent male backside. Charly still didn't know which view she preferred. Will walking in was just as appealing to her as when he was walking away.

"He didn't kiss you goodbye," Tammy said.

"Why would he?" Charly made herself laugh off the image. She couldn't indulge in that little fantasy at work. "We're just friends. And this is a workplace."

"Not from where I'm standing, and so what?" Tammy flung a hand toward the spot where Will had been moments ago. "That man wants to sleep with you."

"Whatever." Charly refused to get her hopes up. So far they'd gone out for beer and pool at the pub up the street and gone bowling once, but she knew how this story ended before she turned the last page. The way it always ended—with one more tempting man in the friend column.

It had been that way her whole life. Part of it was being built more like a boy than a woman, but her business played a part, too. Binali Backcountry, her life's passion, took up the majority of her energy and time. She enjoyed the mountains, the risk and reward she could find there, and she rose every morning eager to share her passion and knowledge with others as the owner, as well as a guide. Her commitment and drive didn't leave much room for romance and relationships.

For as long as she could remember, she'd been drawn to the wild call of the mountains and canyons surrounding the Four Corners Monument. Born and raised just outside of Durango, she'd spent her life exploring until it all felt as personal as her own backyard. Her grandfather often boasted that you could drop her anywhere on the planet and she'd find her way home no matter the weather or resources. She could track and mimic any animal that called this area home and, more importantly, she could find lost people better than any bloodhound.

Typically, men looking for a good time didn't put those skills at the top of the list when they wanted a date. Or a girlfriend. It was too soon to tell if Will would be different. She returned to the office to print out the work schedule.

Looking it over as it came off the printer, she prepared for the inevitable complaints. She required all of her guides to spend a few hours in the shop each week. It wasn't a popular stance and she'd lost a few good guides to nearby competitors since she'd implemented the policy. No one loved getting out and guiding mountain and canyon tours more than she did. But it was important to her that everyone understood the gear they carried for customers and that selling tours was a group effort. It kept them all invested and focused on the overall success of Binali Backcountry. As she'd explained it—again—at last month's staff meeting, no one sold a tour better than the guide who loved to lead it.

The reverse was also true, and it was past time for Tammy to get out and away from the business district. "Have you decided which tour you'll join next week?"

Tammy cringed and busied herself with a sudden interest in the day's few credit card receipts. "I'm not sure my boots are broken in yet."

Charly glanced at Tammy's feet and noted the cute Western boots better suited for line dancing than hiking. "So start small. How about something down around Lake Nighthorse or along the river trail?" Those routes naturally had a slower pace, more photo opportunities and generally left people delighted rather than exhausted.

"Maybe." Tammy popped her gum while she flipped through the appointment book. "Clint only has openings on his two-night thing into the canyon."

Ah. Now Charly had the clear picture. Tammy was crushing on Clint. The girl had good taste, but Clint Roberts wasn't the one-woman kind of guy, and she didn't want Tammy's feelings getting hurt in the bargain.

"I know the tents are rated to thirty below or whatever," Tammy said, "but I can't believe that material is really effective."

"What you should believe," Charly said, her voice calm but stern, "is that your job here depends on you getting outside by next week."

Tammy's eyes went wide, shimmering with tears. "That's not fair."

This kind of thing was exactly why Charly preferred working with men. No emotional games, just the occasional posturing, and she knew how to shut that down. Charly took a calming breath, reminded herself the tears were an act, a tool Tammy had probably learned to wield early in life. "That was the deal when I hired you. Do I need to pull out the paperwork you signed?"

"No." Tammy's tears evaporated instantly.

"I'll go with David on the river trail tomorrow. Unless…"

Charly was half-afraid to ask. "Unless what?"

"What if I took over the office stuff? All that computer crap you hate is a piece of cake for me."

"Really?"

Tammy nodded, hope clearly bubbling over as she laced her fingers and bounced a little.

Charly glared at her. "Why didn't you say something when I was ready to put a tent stake through the computer last week?"

"And miss a chance to stare at Will's ass?"

Valid point. The girl had priorities, even if they were different from Charly's. "You still have to take the tours." She held up a hand, cutting off Tammy's protest. "At least the ones close to town. It will help you sort out what treks appeal to what type of person."

"Okay, okay." Tammy shook back her cloud of perfect, bottle-blond hair. "But if I fall in the river you'll be on your own with the computer stuff."

"I'll tell David to be extra careful with you."

"Thank you." She tapped her fingernail on the counter. "You know, I could even put the tour schedules into a calendar app and then all of you would know what's what out on the trails."

She and her guides already knew that, but

Charly appreciated the effort. "I'd go with that in a heartbeat if—"

"Right," Tammy interrupted. "Cell reception is crappy in the wild. One more reason to appreciate the city."

"Takes all kinds to keep the world turning." Charly flipped through the mail, finding an official envelope from the park service between the catalogs and handing the rest of the stack to Tammy. She ripped it open, pleased to find a check for her latest consulting work. "I'm going to run this over to the bank."

"I'll hold down the fort."

Charly breathed deep of the clear, crisp air as she strolled down the block. It always felt good when a consulting job had a happy ending. This time around it had been a weekend hiker who hadn't come back on schedule. At the twenty-four-hour mark, his wife had insisted the park service start a search and they in turn had called Charly. When they reached him, they'd found the poor guy had taken a tumble and lost his radio. Easy enough to do this time of year when the weather couldn't decide between winter and spring.

Up ahead, she saw Will on his route, but he was chatting with the owner of the pub where they had shared their first beer. The man was too easy on the eyes, and she purposely looked away, just to prove she could. It wouldn't do her any good to get attached to the idea that he would see her as more than a pal with breasts. She glanced down at her chest. Her barely B cups might not be big enough to meet the general definition. They certainly had never been big enough to change the way the local guys saw her.

Tammy might be right about the raw chemistry between Charly and Will, and Charly was definitely ready to see where pheromones and attraction could lead. How could she find out if Will was on the same page? She was darn sure ready for more than another buddy to talk beer, guns and trails.

She yanked open the bank door and stutter-stepped to avoid bumping into the police officer walking out. "Whoops. Sorry, Steve."

"No problem. How are things?"

"Can't complain," she replied. "How are the kids?"

"Good." He stepped back inside with her. "I'm thinking about taking my youngest down into the canyon when it warms up a bit."

Steve had worked part-time for her father during their senior year. They'd gone to the homecoming dance—as friends—because both of them had been too busy that season to find real dates. Suddenly she felt seventeen and awkward again, remembering the time they'd driven out to prep a campsite in the canyon and stayed long into the night, watching a meteor shower from the back of his pickup truck. She'd wished for a kiss as the stars fell, but Steve didn't oblige.

Thank God, she thought now. It would've been weird. More of an experiment than romance, even under that endless sky.

Steve waved his hand in front of her face. "Charly? You okay?"

With a little jump and a self-conscious smile, she apologized. "Just lost in thought." Steve's youngest daughter had recently discovered a new fascination with photography. "Take her into the canyons southeast of town and she can get some amazing sunset pictures."

"That's a great idea. She'll love that. I'm glad I bumped into you."

"Me, too. Have a great time."

They went their separate ways, leaving Charly feeling half a step out of sync with the rest of her world as she made the deposit. It irritated her. She had exactly what she wanted. More. With the business she had freedom and plenty of time in wide-open spaces, challenges of every variety. She had exactly what she needed, sharing the world she loved from mountaintop to river to canyon with new people every day.

"Living the dream," she reminded herself as

she walked back up the block to the Binali Back-country storefront. This was her heritage as well as her dream come true.

So why did it feel as though something was missing? Determined to adjust her attitude, she tipped her face to the snowcapped peaks kissing the horizon. This happened to her when she spent too much time in the office and not enough out in the field. Four days was about her tolerance for the city life, and she hadn't led a tour in over a week. Well, easy enough to fix that. She'd just make time for an early hike tomorrow morning since she had plans tonight. Plans with a man she definitely wanted to know better. In the biblical sense rather than strictly as a friend. Maybe she should ask Tammy for pointers on how to stage a seduction. Heck, she needed pointers in how to tell if a guy was open to being seduced.

She was laughing at herself, her balance somewhat restored, when she strolled back into the store.

"Must have been some check," Tammy said.

"Every little bit helps," she admitted.

"I opened the fan mail while you were gone."

"We got fan mail?"

"Sure." Tammy spun a handwritten note card around for Charly's inspection. "Take a look."

Charly read it aloud, happily recalling her

time with the Ronkowski family. "'Thanks again for making our vacation something we'll remember forever. The kids are still talking about it with anyone who will stop long enough to listen. We've been camping and taken tours through all kinds of places, but Charly, your expertise and passion for the area made all the difference. We're already planning to return to Colorado and take another tour with you this summer.'"

The note went on, elevating Charly's mood with every word. She'd led the parents and their three kids on a camping excursion through the canyon she'd recommended to Steve earlier. "Wow. We can pull a few of these lines for the website," she said. In fact, she wanted to upload the new quotes right this second. "They were a fun family."

"They sure think the world of you."

"It's easy to share what you love best." An idea dawned, one she thought might be a good compromise for Tammy. "Want to go hiking with me tomorrow?"

"What? And close the store?"

"No. Before we open. Before breakfast."

Tammy's jaw dropped open. Then she snapped it shut and glared at Charly. "This is some kind of test."

"Not at all." Charly gathered up the mail as

she rounded the counter, smiling again at the note from the Ronkowskis. "I just need to get outside."

Tammy pointed at the door with her perfectly manicured finger. "You just came in."

Charly laughed. "I meant the *big* outside, away from sidewalks and storefronts."

"You're a nature addict." Tammy shook her head, as if the diagnosis were fatal. "I have plans for tomorrow before breakfast."

"You do?"

"Yup." Tammy nodded emphatically. "Sleep."

"Fine." Unable to argue with a confirmed city girl, Charly ducked into the office to deal with a few remaining administrative details. If she lingered, she knew she'd ask Tammy for advice about men and that just felt too…needy, she decided.

She'd let the mysterious chemistry work, and whatever happened with Will happened.

WILL TOOK A final look around his apartment and decided he had everything set for his movie date with Charly. The clutter was gone, the kitchen and bathroom spotless. The beer was cold, he had microwave popcorn ready to go, and he'd bought a pack of cupcakes for dessert. Yeah, he had everything except the movie.

Binali Backcountry had quickly become the

high point on his postal route each day. During his first week on the job, chatting up so many strangers all at once had left him drained and craving nothing more than hours of quiet at the end of the day. Then he'd met her. There was an ease about Charly that smoothed him out. He blamed it on the absolute confidence that hovered over her like a cloud. That particular trait wasn't something he saw in most civilians.

Casey expected Will to get involved here, so sticking to his hermit tendencies wasn't an option even for personal time. Following orders, Will had jumped in with both feet and asked her out, telling himself it was all part of burrowing deep into the cover story.

Being a mailman came easily enough. The tasks were so different from his military career, he appreciated having the mental space to assess the community. The people were nice and generally took pride in the area as a whole. He'd been right about the mile-wide streak of independence out here. While it had been hard work denying the part of him that needed solitude and quiet, he was making the adjustment.

I'm dating, he thought, checking his watch. Charly would be here in ten minutes. He picked up the remote and started scrolling through his extensive movie library. He'd picked up most of the titles during his time on bases where the troops had created dedicated servers packed with entertainment for relaxation between missions. Still, he couldn't make up his mind about what they should watch tonight.

This was the first time they were staying in, which felt like enough pressure, but he didn't know her tastes well enough to make a confident choice. Will decided to narrow the list to three and let her make the final call.

While he skimmed through the long list, his cell phone sounded with the old-school telephone ring he'd programmed for contact from Director Casey. The familiar anticipation of a mission shot through his system as he answered. "Chase here."

"This is a high-alert notification."

Thank God, some action. He was more than ready for a challenge bigger than movie selections.

"We have confirmed reports that a device known as a Blackout Key, a cutting-edge cyber weapon, has been stolen," Director Casey explained. "It's reverse-engineering software. I'm told the damn thing can breach everything from bank systems to nuclear weapon launch codes."

Will took a slow breath and waited for more details. Software could hide anywhere, on anyone.

It could be as sexy as a tube of lipstick or

as unassuming as a car key. Hell, something like that could hover up in a technology cloud, just waiting for the right bad guy to access it. He fought the immediate disappointment. He couldn't hunt software. Not the way he hunted bad guys.

Still, he wondered how it tied in to Durango. Every business on his route relied on software security and the internet in some capacity. Thinking of the businesses on his route, he automatically prioritized them, starting with the prime targets. The two banks for sure, but he could see the value in targeting the investment group and a nationally recognized architectural firm, too.

"Three suspects were under surveillance," Casey continued, "but one suspect, a man we believe was instrumental in the key's development, has suddenly disappeared from the Los Angeles area. The files and everything related to the program have vanished from all databases in the DC lab."

"Am I being relocated?" The flicker of regret at leaving Durango—and Charly—surprised him. His SEAL training had made him innately qualified for action in this kind of rugged terrain.

"No. You sit tight. This is a nationwide alert. What we don't have yet is hard intel on the location of the key. Photos of the missing suspect and full details will be emailed to you. Keep the information secure and notify me at once if you spot anything that relates to this alert."

"Sit tight," Will echoed. "Does that mean you don't want me to act?"

Casey hesitated. "You are authorized to take whatever action is necessary to protect civilians or recover the Blackout Key. This breach cannot go public. We can't allow it to reach the black market, either."

"Copy that."

The line went dead, and a moment later a knock sounded at the door. He set the phone to vibrate and pushed it into his back pocket. When he opened the door, the rich aroma of hot pizza spiced the air.

Charly smiled at him over the big square box. Her long hair, usually pulled back from her face in a braid or ponytail, was down tonight. It fell like a thick midnight curtain across her shoulders and lower, brushing the gentle curve of her breasts highlighted by the deep V of her light green sweater. His breath caught and his stomach growled.

"Sounds like I'm just in time." Her lips gleamed with a soft sheen, and she'd added some subtle touch that made her big brown eyes wider, more… It hit him suddenly—she'd applied makeup. For him. He liked it.

"You look great," he said, stepping back so she could come inside. She looked more delicious than any meal. He reminded himself they were friends. The smart play was to take it slow. His assignment was long-term and he didn't want to make the wrong move and alienate her—or anyone else.

While she settled the pizza in the kitchen, he pulled down plates and offered her a choice of the locally crafted beers he'd picked up.

His phone hummed, and he pulled it out. A quick check of the display confirmed it was the expected information from Casey.

"Problem?"

"Not tonight," he said, raising his glass to hers for a toast. "Let's eat."

Chapter Three

The next morning, under a cloudless blue sky, Charly parked her truck behind the store and slid the key into the back door. Stepping inside, she silenced the alarm system and locked the door behind her. At just past seven, she still had two full hours before Tammy arrived.

She sighed happily. Two full hours to enjoy the sweet high resulting from the combination of an interesting evening with a sexy man and a perfect morning hike through crisp winter air.

It had been a bit more challenging than she'd anticipated getting out of bed after the impromptu double feature at Will's place. The beer and pizza had been impeccable accompaniment for the loud, over-the-top action flick they'd started with. But his unexpected admission that he had a weakness for Disney films had forced her to test his honesty. She'd woken up with random lyrics and lines from *The Little Mermaid* playing in her head.

Along with the memory of his face—so solemn—when he'd said the film had been required viewing during his navy training. She'd laughed in complete disbelief over both parts of his wild claim.

Oh, he undoubtedly had the well-honed body of a warrior, but she couldn't fathom any reason a navy veteran would settle in Colorado. She'd blurted out the observation and listened, entertained by his colorful explanation of having had his fill of endless oceans and major waterways.

Whatever the reason, she was more than glad he was part of her landscape now. "You've got it bad," she scolded herself while she started a pot of coffee. A few dates was way too soon to be this enthralled over any man, but especially irresponsible when the man was new to town.

Still, she'd wanted to spin in a happy circle as she left his place last night, after he'd asked her for a pool game rematch at the pub tonight. This was almost like having a boyfriend, though they hadn't really discussed it in those terms.

She suffered another nearly deflating moment thinking the feelings were only on her side, but then she remembered the way he'd looked at her when she left last night. There'd been a certain chemistry—or at least something that felt distinctly warmer than friendship in his clear blue eyes.

Catching her reflection in the glass of the half door between the storefront and the back room, she wondered what Will saw when he looked at her. She paused, taking stock. With her hair pulled back from her face, a company ball cap on her head and only a sweep of mascara, she felt plain. Bland.

Not ugly, just...unfinished. *Unpolished* was the better word. But she had no intention of changing her habits. Makeup didn't go well with her career, though Will had seemed to approve of her effort in that area last night. She wasn't sugar and spice and everything curvy and nice like other women. A total tomboy, she'd spent her youth proving she could keep up with the nature-loving men in her life instead of embracing the critical differences that made her a woman, from chewing tobacco—once, on a dare—to splitting wood every winter. It was simply who she was. She wouldn't change for any man, no matter how hot and ripped or funny or intriguing. With an irritated huff for letting anything as silly as a reflection erode her good mood, she pushed through the door and into the storefront.

She hit the power button for the computers, then went out and took a quick stock of the displays. Tammy had everything neatly organized, and while she might not be a big fan of the great outdoors, she was an asset here in the shop.

"Here's hoping she's that efficient with spreadsheets, schedules and financials."

Charly filled a tall mug with coffee and returned to her desk, the same simple and scarred desk her father and grandfather had used. Now it was hers. Feeling connected to all they'd handed down to her, she started on the email.

She discarded the obvious spam and answered the easy ones before dealing with the rest of it. Inquiries ranged from advertising offers to shipping confirmations. A new shipment of ball caps was scheduled to arrive today, and she smiled when she saw they were coming by the US Postal Service. She'd make herself available to sign for that package when the hunky new mailman delivered it.

The time slipped away as she dealt with necessities and soon she heard the security system chiming as someone came in the back door. Her eyes went to the little monitor perched on the corner of her desk that kept an eye on the back entrance. Tammy and Clint.

Well, that should keep spirits high around here today. Charly stood up, stretching her arms and grabbing her empty coffee cup to go greet them.

After catching up and successfully dodging direct questions about her evening, she shared one of the more intriguing email messages with Clint.

"Take a look," she said, handing over the page she'd printed out. "It's a team-building thing. Sounds like we can name our price."

Clint gulped his coffee while he read the short message. One of her father's hires, Clint had joined Binali Backcountry almost on his first day in Durango. Blond, lean, with sun-kissed skin and deep dimples, Clint was a good-looking guy, and she understood Tammy's wistful crush on him.

But Clint had his own priorities. When he'd invited Charly to dinner, it had been for the sole purpose of learning all he could about the trails she'd been running tame on her whole life.

She valued his friendship, work ethic and love of the job. When Charly's father stepped back from the business, Clint stepped up, helping her maintain the reputation of excellence. And as each of her brothers followed their careers away from Durango, Clint had filled the void, becoming an important partner and friend.

"Says he'll be in this afternoon." Clint set the printed email aside in favor of a fast-food bag of breakfast. "Want me to be here?" He stuffed a big bite of a breakfast sandwich into his mouth.

Charly cut short the urge to tease and judge him. For a man comfortable eating off the land, he made up for it whenever he had the chance. "Something like this will take two guides for sure."

He nodded, chewing thoughtfully. "What are you thinking of charging?"

She tossed out a number. "Plus the rental gear."

Tammy whistled, but Clint's eyebrows dipped low. "For seven software geeks in this weather? Add in another grand for pain and suffering."

"You charge the *customer* for the chance to suffer?" Tammy was aghast.

"No, darlin'." Clint's dimples showed up. "That's for *our* pain and suffering. Desk jockeys tend to whine."

"I wouldn't whine," Tammy vowed.

"I'd never give you cause," Clint said, his voice oozing charm and innuendo.

Charly rolled her eyes. Tammy looked as though she might dissolve into a puddle. "Why don't you unlock the front door," she instructed Tammy. Clint had no idea the destruction his little flirtation could leave behind.

"Come on," she said to Clint. "Let's hammer out a few ideas and price points. We can give them options."

"You really don't want to risk losing them, I

guess," he said, following her to the office. "But our books can't be that dire."

"They're not. We're doing great," she assured him.

Clint pushed aside some catalogs, making room for his coffee cup on a corner of her desk. Settling back in the only other chair, he finished off his breakfast while they came up with a few package ideas.

"Seems sudden," he said when she was printing out the varied proposals.

"What do you mean?" She shot him a look as he worked the wrapper of his meal into a ball between his palms. A sure sign he was thinking.

"Come on. You think this guy just plans to hand out plane tickets when his crew comes in today or do you think they've been in on the planning process?"

"Does it matter? The email says they just wrapped a project. They want to cut loose and get out of the office."

"In their place I'd go to Vegas."

"Then be grateful they're coming here and want to give us their money."

"If you close the deal, I've got plenty of ways to spend my cut." Clint flipped through the pages once more. "Should we pad that pain-and-suffering number a little more?"

"There's padding and then there's outright greed."

His dimples flashed again. "True." He leaned forward, his eyes twinkling. "But if they go the mountain route, they'll be *cold*." He stood, pretending to shiver. "We could make a side bet that you'll cave to the inevitable whining before I do."

"No deal," she said on a chuckle. "I can be just as much a hard-ass as you when it's necessary."

Clint scoffed. "Then start practicing, sister, and get the payment up front." He clapped her on the shoulder. "I've got a feeling these soft, cube-withered geeks will have us earning every penny once they get a taste of nature up on the mountain at this time of year."

"You're a cynic." She shooed him out of the office with orders to make space in the back room for the delivery coming in. "And put some polish on your professional charm while you're at it."

A FEW HOURS LATER, as she listened to their potential new client, she realized both she and Clint were right. The job would be lucrative, but with every passing minute it was becoming more complicated.

"Let's do this," Charly suggested to the client.

"Which of the options presented comes closest to what you have in mind?"

Reed Lancaster had made it clear from the moment he'd walked in that money was no object. His precise though relaxed appearance gave her an impression of significant wealth to back up the statement. His cashmere sweater, perfectly creased and cuffed khaki slacks and stylish shoes told the story. She imagined he spent a small fortune to keep his hair trimmed, and the gray at his temples added distinction. It was pointless to guess how much he'd shelled out for the Rolex on his wrist. She hoped he had the sense to leave it in his hotel safe rather than wear it on the excursion they were planning. Now, if they could just agree on where he wanted to go and the top three objectives he wanted to get out of the hike.

"As I explained in the email, my team deserves a break. I want to build on our momentum and camaraderie. The three-day hike into the mountains sounds ideal."

"We'll make sure your team is bonding while they're having fun," Clint said.

Mr. Lancaster ignored him, focusing on the paperwork in front of Charly. "Ms. Binali, I've done the research, read the reviews and asked around since coming to town two days ago. Your company has a reputation as the best."

He removed his reading glasses—no drugstore cheaters for Mr. Lancaster, these were designer frames.

"Your specific reputation—" he looked directly at Charly "—is what brought me here." He tapped the small table. "I've taught everyone who works for me that to settle—on anything—is equal to defeat. With every project, every day, we strive for excellence. We are the team that sets the bar others try to reach. I won't give them less than the best experience possible. That means I need you."

"I appreciate the vote of confidence." She gave him a smile and while she gathered the proposals into one stack, putting her favorite mountain hike option on top based on his decision, Mr. Lancaster reached into his coat and withdrew a long, slim wallet.

He'd said there were two hobby photographers on his team. While there wasn't a bad view on any of the routes she and Clint had chosen, Lancaster insisted on the mountain options despite the weather risks.

"The mountains will give you stunning views, crisp air and opportunities for teamwork from the campsites to the hike itself." She forced herself to keep talking as he counted out cash. "You're sure everyone on your team can handle the physical exertion?"

He added more bills, hundreds, she noticed, to the stack. "Fitness is another requirement to stay on my team, Ms. Binali."

"All right." The guy struck her as a tough boss. It would be interesting to meet the people who chose to work with him. "Clint and I will get things together."

Lancaster's gaze slid to Clint and back to hers. "You're sure two guides are necessary?"

She willed Clint to keep his mouth shut. "Two guides will guarantee you and your team get the most out of the excursion and the challenge course experiences we'll provide."

Lancaster dipped his chin in silent acknowledgment, though his lips were pressed into a thin line. "What needs to be signed?"

She offered the basic waiver and contract and explained the maps on the page, highlighting the parking and load-out areas. "We can meet at eight—"

"We'll start at seven o'clock. Tomorrow."

The customer is always right. It took a few repetitions to believe it. "Okay, we can do that," she agreed reluctantly. "This is the list of gear and waivers for each member of your team. I'll need them back by—"

"I have them here," he said, cutting her off again. He opened a leather portfolio and produced the documentation for each of the six people on his team. All men, she noticed, though he hadn't specified that detail. "I printed them from the website to save time. The photos were cropped from our company picnic last year."

She handed the pages to Clint, who skimmed them and gave her a small nod, confirming the required information and signatures were all in order.

"We won't need rental gear," Lancaster added. "Everyone has been outfitted according to the resources posted online."

Efficiency must go along with being the best, she thought. She couldn't fault him. Those lists covered the basics and were up-to-date. "Does that include tents and personal camping gear?"

"Yes."

"Great." She tried to show some excitement, but Lancaster's rigid determination to have everything his way got under her skin. The increasing profit margin should make Clint happy. "Does anyone on your team have food allergies?"

Mr. Lancaster shook his head.

"Then it seems we're set. Binali Backcountry will provide the necessary gear for the team challenges." She wanted to be absolutely clear on that point. It was standard procedure, for convenience as well as liability. Relieved he didn't try to convince her he was bringing that along, too, she stood. Lancaster and Clint followed suit and they all shook hands. Since she hadn't been expecting to head out tomorrow, she'd need the rest of the evening for preparation.

"He's a tough bastard," Clint murmured, watching Lancaster climb into a glossy Mercedes crossover parked across the street. "You think that's a rental?"

Charly picked up the stack of cash and counted it. "For that guy? No way." She shook her head. "He probably bought it just for this trip."

"Is the money real?"

"Yes," she said with a tight laugh, retreating to her office. "Can you get started on the gear and packing?" Clint nodded, leaning against the doorjamb. "Great. Thanks." It was short notice, but just as Mr. Lancaster had said, Binali was the best. They could make this happen. "I'll send Tammy to make the deposit and pick up groceries."

"Sure thing. Just as soon as the mail comes," Tammy replied absently as she flipped through the waivers and photos, putting the information into the folder that indicated a booked excursion. "The best part of this job is getting a daily dose of superhunk."

Clint's face clouded over as he turned to face Tammy. "Lancaster? He's old enough to be your father."

"First, age is only a number," she scolded. "Second, ick," Tammy finished with a mock shudder. "I meant the mailman. The Lancaster dude is way too uptight for me. Good luck with him on the mountain."

"We'll be all right," Charly said. "He paid cash, all of it up front, and I know we'll surpass his expectations." She ignored the unanimous eye rolling. "Come on, both of you. Get busy. I have a schedule to adjust."

Clint disappeared into the back, and her butt had barely landed in her desk chair when she heard the chime on the front door. Judging by Tammy's warm greeting, Will had arrived with the day's mail.

Charly paused long enough to hit Print for the standard grocery list and then walked out to join the conversation. Tammy had signed for the box, her fingers tracing the corners while she flirted shamelessly with Will. Charly told herself it didn't matter. Tammy could enjoy the view of Will's body, but she sure as hell wasn't Will's type.

The catty assessment startled her as Charly watched them. What did she know of Will's type? Technically, she didn't have a claim on the man. They'd only been out on a few friendly dates. They hadn't even exchanged any romantic physical contact yet.

"Hey there, Charly." Will's smile lit up his silver-blue eyes.

"Hi." Her knees felt weak. How silly. "Having a good day?"

"Good enough." He nodded to the big box he'd set on the counter. "New gear?"

"Ball caps," she said. "We sell them—" she tipped her head toward the display in the front window "—but we give them to our guests. A gift-with-purchase kind of thing."

"The bright colors must make it easy to do a head count."

"You'd be right about that." She turned to Tammy. "I have the list and deposit ready to go."

"Cool." Tammy accepted the bank bag and the grocery list. "On account?"

"Please."

"You got it. I'll just take this back to Clint. Have a great day," Tammy said, aiming a wink at Will.

"She's got a little crush going on," Charly explained.

"On me?" Will's dark eyebrows winged up.

"On men in general, I think." She appreciated his quick laugh. "But I meant she has a crush on Clint. At least this week."

Will looked mildly relieved. "Hope that works for her. Are we still on for pool tonight?"

Charly winced. "Sorry. I have to take a rain

check. We picked up a new client determined to squeeze every minute out of his tour, starting bright and early tomorrow morning." She tapped the stack of waivers on the counter. "Some bigwig software guy with more money than sense wants a team-building excursion. Clint and I need to prep."

Will glanced at the paperwork and then raised his gaze back to her. "No problem," he said easily. "We'll make up for it when you're back."

His smile looked sincere, but she wondered if she'd shown enough regret about canceling. She stopped before the analysis paralyzed her and turned her into a babbling dork. If she wanted something different with Will, she'd have to behave differently than she had with other guys. "Maybe you should practice your bank shots while I'm away," she said. Did that come out as a challenge or as the flirtation she'd meant it to be?

He rested his forearms on his side of the counter, bringing himself closer to eye level with her. "Maybe I threw the game last time we played."

She licked her lips, watched his eyes follow the move. "Maybe I don't believe you."

"Would you believe I was distracted by the view?"

Oh, my. Her throat went dry. She desperately wanted that to be true. Just as she wanted to believe she could take some time to play a couple games of pool with him tonight and still get things ready on time, but she knew better. "I really hate that we'll have to wait to find out," she said at last, uncertain of the next step in the game.

He stood tall and gifted her with a smile guaranteed to keep her warm over the next three nights sleeping in a tent near the cold summit of the mountain. In that instant, she was determined to give him good reason to aim that sexy smile her way more often.

"I'll get back to my route and leave you to it."

"Okay." She did a mental eye roll at that profound comeback. "I'll see you as soon as I get home," she added as he reached the door.

"Can't wait." He pushed the door open and paused. "Be safe, Charly."

The gravity of his tone, the concern in his eyes, turned her mute. She stared as he left and passed the window. He looked back, caught her watching, and waved.

She managed to return the gesture before his long stride propelled him down the street.

"Whoa," Tammy said from behind her. "I thought the store might catch on fire from the sparks flying."

Not likely. But the comment made Charly feel better. She couldn't quite believe the attraction and chemistry went both ways. "I thought you were out on errands," she muttered, flipping through the stack of envelopes Will delivered.

"And miss that? No way."

Charly had to laugh it off, resisting the urge to ask Tammy for how-to advice on men. "We both need to get busy," she said and turned for her office. "We barely have enough time as it is." It would take a concentrated effort to keep her mind on the details. She promised herself the reward for her focus now meant she could daydream about Will on the hike tomorrow.

Chapter Four

Will had spent the early-morning hours before his shift reviewing the full intel and reports from Director Casey. The capabilities of the Blackout Key Casey had outlined in the brief phone call were the tip of the iceberg.

The more he'd read and uncovered about Reed Lancaster, created a different kind of chill. If Lancaster had somehow pulled off this theft, if he had the key, this situation would get ugly in a hurry.

The man had an ax to grind with the top-level players in the technology and software development food chain. For years Lancaster had been outspoken, the proverbial squeaky wheel demanding justice from the companies he claimed had stolen his cutting-edge work and tossed him out without so much as a severance package. According to the file, Lancaster didn't just want the Blackout Key, the damned thing was his brainchild. Though it had gone through several development stages and was most recently funded by a government research group, the technology was his creation. While nothing proved he had it, a fully developed, working version of the key could help Lancaster strike back at his perceived enemies. If he did that—and succeeded—the security protocols that protected the nation would fall like dominoes.

As Will studied the file, Lancaster's outspoken threats didn't bother him nearly as much as the recent silence. Men didn't preach vengeance with such intense venom, only to walk away from it without any logical explanation. Not without a settlement or gag order. Will had combed the internet and the files and found no sign of either scenario involving Lancaster.

He'd had all of that rattling around in the back of his mind as he'd started his mail route, wondering what might bring a man like that to Durango. Nothing in the file suggested Lancaster could satisfy his revenge here, which made it more surprising when he'd spotted Lancaster's face on a picture attached to a Binali Backcountry liability waiver as he'd delivered Charly's mail.

The man hadn't bothered with an alias. Bold. In Will's experience that kind of bold meant all kinds of trouble. As he continued along his route, he prioritized the next steps: notify Casey, get a net over Lancaster. Good thing he knew where to find him. As long as Lancaster didn't get spooked before meeting Charly for the hike in the morning.

Hard to believe Lancaster suddenly wanted to commune with nature. It didn't make any sense. What was he after in the mountains? Nothing good, Will decided.

He stalked up the street, his nice-guy postman smile on his face, all the while knowing he couldn't let Charly just walk out into the wilderness with Lancaster. The man and the—missing—Blackout Key he'd envisioned were wanted by nearly every federal agency in the nation. He laughed at the irony. It was possible the postal service was the only agency that hadn't been alerted to the problem.

He spent the rest of his route brainstorming ideas to close in on the target. It would've been weird if he'd asked to go along. Charly would never let her new pal, the friendly mailman, tag along as an extra on what promised to be a tough three-day exercise. She had no way of knowing he could handle things as well as anyone on her staff. He needed more information about the client, the tour and who was going along, but she'd canceled their dinner and now he didn't have easy access.

Logistically, he couldn't tag along even if he

wanted to. It wasn't an option to take time off from the day job. He hadn't accrued any personal days yet and maintaining cover and operation security protocol was essential to his long-term success here.

Instinct and responsibility battled inside his head as he chatted with people on his route. This new development had popped up sooner than he'd expected out of this current assignment. To be effective he had to do more than protect Charly from Lancaster. He had to approach this with a big-picture perspective. But she was leading a man wanted for questioning into the mountains and giving Lancaster too many options to avoid the authorities.

Casey would expect details, and Will wanted to give them to him. In between the stops on his route, Will sent a short text message up the line. The response was no surprise: he was tasked with observing Lancaster, but ordered not to interfere until he knew why the man was in Colorado.

Fine. Will understood how to follow orders during compartmentalized operations. It didn't take three guesses to know what the boss was thinking: Lancaster had come to Durango for the key. So why hire Charly? An exchange of some sort had to be involved. He slowed his pace and tried to look tired. Anything to make it more believable when his boss got the call tomorrow that Will was down with a late-season case of the flu.

HOURS LATER, AS the first evening stars lit the sky over the mountains, Will's new Jeep managed the rugged drive between the highway and the Binali property with no problem. When he'd bought the car, he'd told himself it was an investment, part of the cover for the job. And he'd been right, but soon discovered he enjoyed the rugged capability of this vehicle as much as he'd enjoyed the sleek, sexy speed of the Corvette he'd left in storage in DC.

She came around the far corner of her house as he parked next to her truck, stopping with her hands on her hips and her head tilted in a silent question.

"Hey," he called out, pushing open his door. "Am I intruding?"

"Not really." Her brow furrowed. "I thought we postponed."

"We did," he agreed with a smile. But he needed information and thought he could do something nice for her in the process. Two birds, one stone. "You have to eat, right?"

"Yeah. I can throw something together, I guess."

She didn't have to say it. He could see he'd

made a mistake, thrown her off by showing up unannounced this way. Nothing to do but go big before she sent him home. "I brought burgers, fries and shakes."

Her face brightened with interest. "Chocolate?"

"Or strawberry. Your choice."

"Hedging your bets?"

"A little," he admitted. "I didn't even eat all the fries on the way over. Do you have time for a break?"

"Sure." She smiled and waved him closer. "Bring it on back."

He grabbed the takeout bags and drinks and followed her around to what appeared to be a small workshop set back from the house.

She cleared space on one end of a table loaded with all kinds of camping gear and then pulled over another stool for him.

Taking a seat, he placed a hot burger and scoop of fries in front of her and scattered a handful of ketchup, mustard and mayonnaise packets between them. "They're both loaded with everything."

"Sounds good. I didn't want to postpone tonight," she said after she'd unwrapped the burger and prepped it her way. "I was looking forward to beating you at pool again."

He laughed as he dragged a fry through the

ketchup he'd puddled on a corner of the foil wrapper. "You said it's an early start tomorrow?"

"We're meeting at six thirty to load up. This guy's serious about getting the most of each and every day."

"Hope you charged him extra."

"Better believe it." She shot him a wink. "My family drummed business sense into me right along with camping and tracking."

He bit off more of the juicy burger, chewing as he looked around the workshop and up toward the mountain peaks before meeting her gaze again. "You've got a nice place out here."

Her lips curved with pride. "I've always thought so."

Stars came to light, more with each passing minute. He hadn't seen a night sky so full since those long nights alone in Afghanistan. "You don't mind being tied so closely to your family?"

"Tied?" She chuckled, brushing salt from her fingers. "It's an honor to carry on what my elders started. Is that why you went into the navy? To get untied?"

Untied. He'd never thought of it like that. "Maybe so." It hadn't started that way. His parents had been proud of him...before things fell apart.

"Hmm. You really should think before you gush on and on like that," she said with a wink.

The urge to explain his decisions surprised him. This was hardly the best time to confess his parents didn't speak to him because his brother had died while following in his military foot-steps. There was never a good time for that story as far as Will was concerned. Besides, he had a job to do here, even if the company was beauti-ful and friendly. "Are you meeting this guy and his team at the main park entrance?"

She nodded. "Clint's meeting me at the shop, then we'll meet the clients at the parking lot." She balled up her burger wrapper and tossed it into the bag. "Clint's so excited about the extra team challenge stuff he probably won't sleep at all tonight."

Will knew the type. He only had to look in the mirror. "I competed in a few challenge course events during my navy days." He'd developed more than a few as a SEAL. He liked the way it felt when her dark eyes skated over his body. "Don't believe me?"

"I believe you," she said, her voice a little breathless. She cleared her throat and slid off the stool to consider the gear spread out on the other end of the long table. "We won't be doing static courses out there."

"Is that some sort of insult?"

"What?" She whipped around, color flooding her cheeks. "No. I would never—"

"Relax." He came to his feet, hands out, palms open. "I was just messing with you. What kind of things does Clint have planned for the group?"

"Probably too many." She rubbed her arms through the thick fabric of the company sweatshirt she wore and sighed. "I didn't mean static courses were any less of a challenge than what we set up during an excursion."

"It's okay," he said, rubbing her shoulder. He was flattered by her concern about offending him. It made him think he had something to look forward to with her after the Lancaster operation was complete.

The powers that be wanted Will to report Lancaster's position, whom he met with and what items or information were exchanged. Apparently, those curious people at the top of the food chain didn't share Will's concern that in order for a man like Lancaster to feel safe about whatever he was up to, anyone who knew about his plans would have to be eliminated.

"I like you, Charly." He blurted it out, immediately wishing he could reel it back in. "I'm sure you've got this under control, but it all sounds sudden and risky."

She shrugged that off, clearly more comfortable with the camping prep than looking at him. "It's sudden, but not risky."

He listened, thinking it was too easy when she

explained the route and the typical places where Clint set up various challenges and teamwork opportunities. "We're not even doing much of the heavy lifting."

"What does that mean?"

She rubbed at her temples, a frown marring her brow. "My client assured me his team is fit and up for anything."

"Is there some reason to doubt him?"

She spread her hands wide and then reached for a hiking pack, stuffing supplies into pockets with an efficiency he admired. "I hope not. For their sake. The route Clint and I are taking isn't for amateurs."

"I'm looking forward to getting out and doing some exploring myself soon." Right now he wished he'd done more than admire the mountains from the convenience of his route. Didn't matter. He'd always found his assigned quarry and survived no matter the odds or terrain.

"David does river hikes a couple of times a week," she said with a wince.

"What's wrong with that?"

"Two things." She balled up wool socks and tucked them into open spaces. "It's water, which you claim to be done with."

"And?" he prompted when she busied herself with the precise attachment of a canteen.

"Tammy is slated to go out on the next tour.

She'd be ogling you the whole time, and I want her to pay attention to the tour."

He laughed. "She ogles me every day."

Charly giggled, then clapped a hand over her mouth. "You know?"

"I'm a mailman, not an idiot."

"Well, you'd be an idiot to invest so much time in your body and not expect some ogling."

"That's a fair point." He sent her a sideways look.

"You think I'm insulting you again."

"No." He stepped closer. "I say what I mean. You don't have to put words in my mouth."

"I'll remember that."

"Do." He kept looking for an opportunity to hide a GPS transmitter on her pack. Based on the route she'd described, she'd be out of cell range before noon tomorrow. "What can I do to help?"

"Dinner was plenty," she said with a shy smile.

He wanted to warn her, but if he said anything, she might telegraph her concerns to Lancaster. While she packed, he made a mental list of things to be aware of on the mountain. He was more than a little relieved when she unlocked a cabinet and pulled out a hefty .38 Special revolver along with ammunition and a flare gun. Not just because it gave him time to put the transmitter on her pack—he felt a little better that she was armed. "Expecting trouble?"

"*Expecting* is a strong word." Her wry smile told him she'd seen her share of the unexpected. "I was raised to be prepared for any emergency. I carry the revolver as a last resort in the case of a wildlife issue."

"Got a snakebite kit?"

"Already packed," she replied, distracted.

He'd been kidding about that. "Isn't it too cold for snakes to be a problem?"

She nodded. "But even when it's cold, snakes can wake up looking for water, so I take it anyway, every time." Her nearly black eyes met his with stark candor. "People do dumb things despite our best advice as guides."

He'd seen the same thing throughout his military career, in every part of the world. "Stupidity is a frequent problem with humans."

"Tell me about it," she said. She looked around the table, but everything was already in her pack. "Mr. Lancaster assures me his team is smart, but there's a big difference between being smart in the office and being smart in the wilderness."

"What's this?" He pointed to the knife she'd set apart from the other items. The dark, hand-tooled leather sheath was a work of art, and the hilt was inlaid with a stunning turquoise mosaic in the shape of a long, elegant feather. His fingers itched to pull it out, to confirm the blade matched the hilt and sheath.

Her face went soft. "A gift from my grandmother. She gave it to me before my first solo hike on Silver Mountain. I don't go anywhere without it." She slid it into her sleeping bag.

"You don't wear it?"

"Sometimes."

He considered pushing her but decided changing the subject was safer. There was more to the knife, more to her history, but she didn't seem inclined to share more right now. "How often do you need the revolver or the flare gun?"

Her sly grin, loaded with self-confidence, brought to mind too many inappropriate, off-topic images. Later, he reminded himself. There would be plenty of time to get to know Charly on a more intimate level later.

"I've only used the flare gun to signal rescuers," she said.

"When you've been lost?"

"No, I signal when I've found lost people." She laughed. "I don't ever recall being lost."

"You're kidding." He leaned back, startled by her claim. He'd been blessed with a perfect sense of direction, as well, which came in handy.

"My grandpa used to say I had a compass where my heart should be."

Will wasn't sure how to respond. It seemed like a backhanded compliment, but he didn't get the impression that Charly was the sort to put up with twisted family dynamics. He had a low threshold for drama, which was why he stayed out of his parents' way. Better for all concerned.

"You think that sounds cold."

"A little."

"He meant it as the highest compliment." She reached over and pulled apart hook-and-loop fasteners with a loud rip.

"I'm all ears."

"Hand me those tent poles."

He did as she asked, waiting patiently for the explanation. Instead, her phone rang, and she pulled it from her hip pocket.

It didn't take long to realize she was speaking with the guide who'd be her partner on tomorrow's hike. The story about her grandfather would have to wait. Will pointed from the tent to the pack, and she gave him a nod, so he finished putting her tent gear into the designated place while he listened to her end of the conversation.

Will didn't know much about Charly's employees, but he assumed she didn't waste time working with anyone subpar. He might've found that reassuring if the circumstances were normal. He made a decision right there. If Lancaster gave Charly and her partner more than they could handle, Will vowed he'd be close enough to clean up the mess.

When she wrapped up her call, he'd get out of her way. He had his own preparations to finish and if he kept asking questions, he was bound to raise her suspicions.

CHARLY WALKED WILL out to his truck, a small part of her wishing the evening didn't have to end so early. Who was she kidding? All of her wanted him to stay longer. "Thanks for bringing dinner by. That was a nice surprise."

"My pleasure." He pulled his keys from his jacket pocket. "I'm glad it worked out."

"Me, too." She nodded, unable to come up with any witty reply. No one but family had ever brought her dinner before a tour or kept her company during the packing. She should tell him that, let him know what it meant to her, but she knew it would come out as a lame thank-you for this or that. Why did she have to suck so badly at this kind of thing?

"Give me a call when you get back?" He opened his car door.

Grateful her lack of feminine wiles didn't seem to put him off, she grinned up at him. In the dark, under all the stars, she let herself fantasize about how it would feel if he kissed her good-night.

She couldn't imagine a better place for a first kiss than out here in the cold night air with the stars as silent, sparkling witnesses.

"Charly?"

"Mmm-hmm."

"You should go inside. Get some rest."

She felt the heat of his hand on her shoulder through the thick layers of her polar-fleece jacket and sweatshirt. The man was like a furnace and she wanted to burrow closer to all that warmth. "Right."

Neither of them moved.

"Drive safe."

His hand slipped away as he pulled out his keys, and she chided herself for missed opportunities. Until he caught her hand. Before she could decide what to do about that, he bent his head and brushed his lips against hers.

A fleeting kiss, over almost before it started, but it rocked her world. "I'll call when I get back," she promised, knowing she was grinning like a fool.

He settled into the driver's seat, his lips tipped up on one side in a cocky smirk. She couldn't find a reason to be annoyed with the expression.

She stayed put, like any girl crushing hard on a boy, and watched until his taillights disappeared down the road. She wasn't sure how she'd get to sleep now, but if she did manage it, she knew she'd dream of Will.

Chapter Five

Charly parked her truck next to Clint's behind the shop and had tossed her pack into the bed when he came out with two tall travel mugs of coffee. "I knew there was a reason I kept you on," she said as he set them in the cup holders.

"Next to you I'm the best guide in the galaxy," he said, boosting up into the driver's seat. "Let's roll."

"You're in a good mood."

"I'm all set." He bobbed his head and rubbed his hands together. "It's gonna be an outstanding day."

There was no reason to doubt him. They were prepared, the client had prepaid in full and when they reached the parking area, she saw Lancaster and his team were gathered around two vehicles, as eager to get started as Clint.

On first impression, Lancaster's team didn't

fit her mental stereotype of software developers. She caught Clint's eye and exchanged raised eyebrows as Clint walked over to double-check their packs and gear. Lancaster hadn't been kidding about his employee standards. Each of the six men addressed Lancaster with quiet respect. She matched each man with the waivers as introductions were made with Bob, James, Scott, Rich, Max and Jeff. Without any protest, all seven guests donned the bright Binali Backcountry ball caps she handed out. The men weren't quite matching, but they'd certainly shopped from the same outdoor outfitter catalog. She counted it a good thing their boots looked broken in, though she'd packed the family remedy for blisters.

"You're all wearing layers as suggested?"

They nodded in unison.

"And you packed rain gear?"

Another nod multiplied seven times. "All right. Clint will give each of you the items you'll carry for the whole party." Next she gave a quick safety briefing. It was standard fare and Lancaster and his team were attentive, but she had the feeling they weren't really tuned in.

Well, that's why I packed the snakebite kit, she thought, leading the party out. Clint brought up the rear as they hiked into the state park along the main road.

Charly made small talk along the way, relieved

when Lancaster and his men responded. Occasionally she walked backward to see how everyone was doing. No one seemed even winded, a good sign, but not typical along the first steep inclines. "Clint packed a thermos of coffee if anyone needs a boost."

"We're fine," Lancaster answered for all of them.

"Great." With a forced smile, she hiked on, pointing out various trees and bird calls. The men were polite, but not excited about any of it. "Clint, can you tell everyone what they can expect at our first stop?"

"Sure."

She listened while her friend explained the first team challenge. The rope bridge exercise sounded ominous, but no one usually suffered more than wet boots. With today's clear weather and a planned stop for a cookout at noon, she hoped the challenge and any possible mistakes loosened up this crew.

Lancaster pulled back his sleeve and checked his watch. "Can we up the pace?"

"Sure," Charly replied, shooting a look at Clint. "If we're all in agreement."

All six men agreed with monosyllabic replies, so she picked up the pace. It put them at the creek ahead of schedule, but maybe that was a good thing. At the wide creek, with the midmorning sunlight bouncing off the water, Clint laid out the supplies and explained the challenge once more.

Lancaster's crew looked at one another, then at the gear at Clint's feet, and finally to Lancaster.

"Make it quick," Lancaster said, checking his watch. He peered up at the cold blue sky while his men started on the exercise.

Clint came over to stand with Charly while the men worked out a solution to cross the water. "If these guys are software engineers, I'm a trained monkey," he muttered for her ears only.

"You brought coffee without a reminder," she pointed out. "I trained you well."

Clint snorted. "Your dad trained me."

She smiled and bumped his shoulder with hers, the easy exchange completely at odds with the tension twisting her stomach. "Family business. I get credit by default." She pulled her water bottle free and took a long drink. Judging by the progress the men were making, they'd be across the stream in less than fifteen minutes. And not one of them would have wet boots.

"What do you think really brought them here?"

Something more than a team-building excursion, she thought, tipping her face to the sunlight. Her grandmother had taught her to pause, to reach out to the world when she needed anything, from her next breath to the answers for a geometry exam. Charly had learned early how to listen to her surroundings. They had options: she could continue on, playing the happy nature guide, or she could confront Lancaster about his real intentions.

"Have I missed something crucial in the news lately?" she asked Clint.

Clint shook his head. "Might be some kind of geocaching team."

That was possible. Except those types didn't usually hire expert guides and they got lost up here frequently enough that Charly was often called in to help find them. "When they complete this exercise, radio back to the store and leave some happy message for Tammy. Tell her to post our progress with this tour to the website."

"She won't be there?"

"Not for another hour or so." Charly raised her phone and snapped a picture of the bridge progress, quickly sending it as a text message attachment before they were out of cell range. Lancaster wouldn't know the store schedule. It might be equivalent to baiting a bear, but if he heard Clint tell someone where they were, it might force him to expose his real plan earlier rather than later.

The man made her nervous, though she couldn't pinpoint why. The sooner she understood what he was up to, the better the odds she could keep everyone safe up here. She watched, considering her options while the team tested the new bridge. One by one, the group crossed over, Charly last.

"That was fun," the man named Scott said, adjusting his pack to sit snug against his shoulders. "Do we take it down now?"

"No. We'll use it on our way back."

"The park service won't be irritated?"

She saw a new opportunity to push at Lancaster's real agenda. "No. They're used to us coming through. This is a standard route for Binali Backcountry."

Lancaster went still, and while she knew it was impossible, it felt as if the air temperature dropped a few degrees. "I requested a unique route."

"And you'll have it," she assured him, infusing her voice with all the patience she could muster. "But there are specific routes on the way in that allow us to get a feel for our clients on each tour."

"I assured you my team is at the peak of fitness."

"You did." She stood still as a tree, the picture of unflappable calm. "And now I know you didn't exaggerate. Thank you."

Lancaster's nostrils flared, his mouth set in a grim line. "I would like to head north, away from established trails so my team has the best experience possible."

She applied balm to her lips while she considered. "And we'll give you that." Capping the balm, she put it back into her jacket pocket. "Better if we stay westbound for a while."

"Why?"

"Heading north right now presents more terrain challenges." She decided not to outline the gulley or the snow-choked pass. She might need one or both of those surprises later, if the situation degraded.

"We can handle any terrain," Lancaster insisted. "I'd like to move north."

She bit back the waspish reply on the tip of her tongue. It wasn't too late to turn this party around and refund his money. He could find another guide, one willing to cave to his impatience. "Mr. Lancaster, my brothers once goaded me into a race to the summit."

"So what?"

Only the memory kept her confident smile on her face. "Determined to win, I took the direct route and learned a hard lesson about variations in terrain."

"We can handle it."

She pulled her sunglasses from her face and planted her hands on her hips. "Mr. Lancaster, if you didn't want an expert guide up here with you, why did you hire me?"

He slid a glance to one of the men behind her. Whatever the response, Lancaster's shoulders relaxed a fraction. "You're right. We've heard so many good things and we all want as much time as possible on the peak itself. The views," he added.

She wasn't fooled. "You won't be disappointed, but questioning my route won't get us there any faster."

"Yes, ma'am." He swept an arm wide, inviting her to lead the way.

She looked at Clint. "Call the shop and let them know the first challenge is done. With flying colors."

"That's not necessary," Lancaster said.

"Of course it is." Charly replaced her sunglasses and set off while Clint obediently left the message they'd discussed. "All part of the service."

Lancaster caught her arm in a hard grip just above her elbow. "This excursion isn't about your publicity, Ms. Binali."

"Let go," she said quietly. When he did, she resisted the urge to rub at the sore spot. She'd have a bruise for sure by tomorrow. "I'm not about to jeopardize my licenses because you want a special, off-the-grid experience."

"But that is exactly what I paid for."

"You're in a national forest, Mr. Lancaster. The geography can't be avoided. There are regulations out here and I *will* stay in compliance for your safety as well as my long-term business interests."

He looked as if he'd argue, maybe grab her again, but one of his men held up a cell phone. "My trail app says snow is on the way tonight."

The announcement didn't make Lancaster happy. "How much?"

"We won't see more than a flurry where we'll be camping tonight," she assured them. "That report is for the upper elevations. We can't get that far today, even with a quick pace."

"Set a quicker pace anyway," Lancaster said.

"You got it." The customer was always right. The philosophy applied to the weird customers, too, as long as their demands didn't put anyone at risk. Charly dialed the pace right up to grueling. Maybe one of his supercapable not-engineers would snap.

Whatever Lancaster was up to, she led them away from easy emergency access and reliable communication. The tactic could backfire, but she trusted her abilities. In fact, with every step away from civilization, her confidence increased. Lancaster had hired the best, but he clearly hadn't considered how that could work against him if he was up to no good.

This part of the world had been her playground all her life. She'd explored it all, from the snowcapped peaks to the canyons to the pueblos farther south. Every step had made her stronger. Every season from birth to present had tied her closer to the land she loved, the land she'd inherited from her elders.

While it helped the business that she was one of the best guides in the area, what mattered more to Charly was sharing what she loved with others. Planting seeds of passion for nature in the hearts of tourists was her personal mission. When people cared about something, when they felt connected, they got involved to protect and preserve. At her grandfather's knee she'd listened to the stories and history of both nature and humans. Her family had taught her everything about the blessings and dangers of the plants and animals in these mountains.

As an adult, when people got lost in what she considered her oversized backyard, she looked at rescue operations as more than a service to one person. She never wanted anyone to hold a grudge against the power of Mother Nature.

Whatever Lancaster had planned—and her

intuition was screaming it wasn't anything good—she wouldn't let him cause lasting problems out here. She'd never purposely led anyone astray on a job, but this might be the time.

The idea didn't sit well, especially since she couldn't be sure whom and what she was dealing with, but patience was another lesson she'd learned the hard way in the great outdoors.

The group was quiet behind her and the back of her neck prickled a warning of Lancaster's hard, unrelenting gaze watching her too closely. She turned often, doing an automatic head count as she kept up her litany about the surroundings, despite the hard pace. It was clear now none of the men were listening. Their loss.

Occasionally she caught a watch or compass check, but nothing was said. She thought maybe Lancaster was settling down until she suggested finding a scenic place to stop for lunch.

He shook his head. "Let's keep moving."

"All right." She carefully stepped around a rotting log. "If everyone agrees."

He dogged her heels. "My team follows my lead. You and your partner work for me now. We'll keep moving."

It had been too much to hope this jerk would give up on the power-play routine. He wasn't the first difficult customer she'd led around the mountain. She stopped short, letting him run into her pack. Her satisfaction didn't last as she did another head count and noticed one of Lancaster's men, Scott, wasn't in sight. Neither was Clint. She scanned the area down the slope, looking for a glimpse of the bright fabric of the company ball caps.

No sign of them. Dread pooled at the nape of her neck and dripped slowly down her spine.

She gripped her radio hard to still her shaking hands and called for Clint. The few seconds before his voice crackled from the speaker were a desperate eternity.

"Just explaining a deer trail," Clint said. "We're all good here."

"I've put you on edge," Lancaster said.

"Yes," she admitted. On edge or not, she was a professional. While Lancaster and his team might be comfortable out here, this wasn't their turf. To a person accustomed to city life, it might look as though she didn't have any recourse or resources out here. She was toying with busting that myth.

"My single-minded focus does that sometimes."

As apologies went, it wasn't good enough. "Putting me on edge isn't healthy for any of us out here." He muttered a better apology, but she wasn't buying it. The bruise on her arm told more truth than any of Lancaster's words. She mentally tossed around defense plans, unable to relax until she saw Clint wave as he and the other man came over the rise. "It might be best if we turn back and you find yourself another guide."

She should've suggested it the moment he'd grabbed her arm. To hell with the money; the business was flush and they were only out groceries and a little gas.

"That's extreme." His smile gave her the willies, made her think of a snake planning to strike. "And it can't really be necessary. My mind is already on our next project and I know our timetable out here isn't adjustable."

"That's easy enough. I'll radio a friend, have them meet us at the campsite tonight and take over from there."

"No. I want *your* guidance, Ms. Binali." He tipped his head toward his team. "We've all been enjoying your lessons today." Behind him six heads bobbed in silent accord. "We're all looking forward to the views from the summit."

Uh-huh. They were looking for something more than a good camera angle and she nearly said so when Clint gave her a hand signal to drop it. Fine. If he was comfortable, she would figure out a way to come to terms with the nerve-racking Mr. Lancaster.

"Considering our progress, I know just the

spot to stop for lunch." She held up a hand when he started to protest. "We *are* stopping for thirty minutes to rest and refuel if you want to reach tonight's campsite safely."

She could tell by his sour expression he didn't agree. A small voice in her head begged him to protest, to push her, so she could leave him out here to manage on his own. That was the threshold, she promised herself. One more argument, one more improper exchange and she and Clint would leave them to find their own way. She'd have to answer for it, and as she trudged on, she imagined the fallout.

Lancaster would, at the very least, post a scathing review online. That kind of thing could be hard to overcome, but one negative review among literally thousands of positives? She refused to worry about that.

No, the fallout from her peers and park rangers concerned her more. While anyone who dealt with tourists understood the occasional desire to throttle someone, abandoning them to the elements was never acceptable. She didn't have anything other than a gut instinct that the men were up to something. While her instincts were respected, the authorities would need more than her hunch and general irritation to justify her leaving a client in the wilderness.

"Hey," Clint said, sidling up to her.

"Hey."

"You're thinking of tossing him into the gulley?"

"Rock slides can be a bitch," she confessed.

"So can gunfire," he whispered, putting an arm around her.

"I wouldn't—" She lost her voice, realizing what he meant. "They're armed."

"I'm betting on rifles instead of tents in the bedrolls. I smelled the gun oil and noticed one ankle holster."

"Damn."

"I agree. And that Max guy?"

"Yeah?" She resisted the urge to look back at the man Clint mentioned.

"He's got a major geek-factor electronic compass disguised as some bogus camera accessory. He's sly about it, but I know what I saw."

Great. Based on Lancaster's insistence to head north, she assumed whatever they wanted was near the summit. Too bad that didn't narrow the possible destination. "What do you want to do?"

"We could ditch them at lunch."

"No." Too risky in broad daylight. "We'll do it tonight." They'd have a better chance of gaining a head start after dark. "We'll split up when they're asleep and you can head down and notify the authorities."

"What about you?"

"I'll circle back and tail them. Find out what they're up to."

"It's a date," Clint said, giving her shoulder a squeeze. Easing away from her, he raised his voice and announced that lunch would be coming up in about a half hour.

Hearing the enthusiastic replies, she wondered if Lancaster was issuing demerits for dissent among the ranks.

She racked her brain for the reason Lancaster and his armed escort wanted to reach the summit. Drugs? Weapons? It could be anything out here, away from prying eyes of civilization.

If Lancaster had come all this way for an illegal meeting or exchange, she didn't hold out much hope he'd leave her and Clint alive to talk about it. With Max's electronic compass and her advice on the best place to make the ascent, Lancaster wouldn't need a guide to get back down the mountain.

It would've been tempting to panic, but Charly wasn't built that way. She'd given him enough of an advantage admitting he made her nervous. That was water under the bridge. She'd use it, let him underestimate her again. It was her best play, because her revolver and a flare gun wouldn't make much of a dent against the arsenal Clint suspected their clients were packing.

Chapter Six

Will had slipped out of his apartment in the middle of the night, geared up for tailing the hikers who were meeting at sunrise. In layers of muted black, the pockets of his cargo pants loaded with the few things he considered essential on an op, he was ready for anything.

The knife in his boot was an upgrade from standard-issue after his original had been used in self-defense during a hostage recovery operation. The modest nine-millimeter semiautomatic handgun in the holster at the small of his back was almost as comforting as having a buddy with him, and it gave give him ample defense—against wildlife or Lancaster.

He had food and ammunition in various pockets, along with gloves, a knit cap, a smaller knife, a flashlight, his cell phone, camouflage paint for his face and, with a nod to Charly's safety concerns, a roll of medical gauze and tape.

Will had done an assessment of the hotel, but

Lancaster had booked rooms at a high-end chain and there hadn't been enough time or an easy way to search the rooms. Instead, he'd stationed himself near the park entrance Charly had mentioned and waited.

The cold didn't bother him; he'd learned to ignore natural circumstances during his SEAL training days. Push-ups and sit-ups in the surf created a new definition for unpleasant. Training was a mind game, teaching the brain and body which details to ignore. Accepting that as fact was the first step to success. Some of the strangest things stuck with him, despite his best effort, and as he'd waited in the dark for Charly and her clients, the soundtrack from *The Little Mermaid* drifted through his head on a repeating loop.

No one seemed to have any good intel why Lancaster had left his California facility. Everyone with an opinion felt it was tied to the Blackout Key, but Casey reported that a search of Lancaster's Los Angeles office and residence hadn't revealed anything new.

There was plenty of proof Lancaster remained obsessed with taking out his industry enemies, but those enemies weren't in the San Juan National Forest. Will hoped being here early would give him a chance to overhear something helpful before Charly led these guys into an area where making an arrest—if necessary—would be next to impossible.

Lancaster had arrived well before Charly, right in line with the personality assessment Casey had provided. The software genius had a compulsive need to be first in all things. Will wondered if it had always been that way, or if that had stemmed from the man's fixation on revenge.

Observing both Lancaster and his team, Will hadn't felt any better about Charly guiding them into the wilderness with only Clint as backup.

This crew clearly had military training. The hair might be longer than regulation, and the clothing civilian, but the six men were hard-core efficient. No wasted motion, no mistakes, no visible distinguishing marks. While he didn't get eyes on any weapons, Will knew they were there. They used such common first names he nearly laughed as he noted them on his arm.

The only clue about their real purpose had been Lancaster's quiet question about the status of a beacon. The reply, from the one they called Max, had been an affirmative nod.

There were all kinds of things that could be attached to a beacon. Anything from software to equipment, even people. Not much to go on, but Will would pass it up the line before he followed them up the trail.

Charly and Clint had pulled into the parking area five minutes ahead of schedule. Smart, considering her client. She had moved with an efficient grace as she helped Clint unload and distribute supplies for the hikers. While she didn't address it, Will knew she caught the general apathy regarding her safety briefing. From his hiding place he grinned, thinking about the snakebite kit. The woman knew her business, even if she didn't know her clients as well as she should this time around.

Between her skill, Clint's assistance and Will trailing the party, he was confident they could manage the situation and prevent Lancaster from crippling national security.

As Charly led them out, Will lagged behind to search the cars. Peering through the window, he saw car rental paperwork tucked in the visors. No shock they were rentals, but this time Lancaster had used an alias. Will used his cell phone to take pictures of the rental agreement and the bar codes on the car windows and emailed the information to Casey's office. Completing all he could here, he hurried to catch up with the hikers.

NOT EVEN THE expertise of the men with Lancaster gave Will much of a challenge as he followed. Too complacent, they clearly didn't sense any threat, which gave him an advantage. He kept them in sight, waiting for some clue about their intentions out here.

Charly's smooth voice carried through the air periodically as she pointed out plants and bird calls, and the occasional track of an animal who'd crossed the trail. Will was sure her typical clients would love it, but Lancaster and his men weren't impressed.

Charly wasn't an idiot; she had to be picking up some vibe that these men weren't here for the scenery and team building. With every exchange—or lack thereof—he grew more concerned that she'd turn the party back before he could figure out what Lancaster wanted.

The pace was quick, but the brisk air felt good in his lungs and his muscles were warm from the exertion. He was starting to understand what Charly found so appealing up here.

Overhearing the disagreement about the route, Will waited until the group moved out of earshot before he called Director Casey. The cell service was sketchy, but he offered the few details he'd gained so far.

"A beacon?"

"That's what he said," Will confirmed. "But no mention of what kind or who or what they were tracking. They were too careful."

"I'll see what I can find out. We're deconstructing the alias."

"Any success?"

"A passport with that name was used four months ago traveling from LAX to France and back."

Will didn't know if that connected with this at all. "The men with him don't have any particular accents."

"He has men with him?"

"Yes. Six." He rattled off the names. "Flawless English, all of them."

"Accents could have been trained out of them."

"True." Will's instincts leaned more toward American mercenaries, carefully researched and quietly recruited to Lancaster's cause. He kept the opinion to himself. Either way, they were armed and dangerous. He was eager to catch up with Charly and keep her safe. "Any ties to Colorado?"

"Not that we've found. We're still looking."

Will understood how manpower and urgency shifted on a daily basis. Based on the file, someone had been dialed into Lancaster's public rhetoric and movements for years. "Any action in his offices?" Everything he'd learned about the reverse-engineering key in the past twenty-four hours made typical hackers look like social butterflies. The data on this sort of software development suggested the potential for abuse was astronomical.

"None. What about the guide?" There was static, and Casey had to try three more times to make the question clear to Will.

"She's solid," Will replied, shifting a bit to find a stronger signal. "The best guide out here."

"Could Lancaster turn her?"

"Into what?" The idea of Charly being influenced to do something illegal amused Will, though he knew everyone had a price. "She doesn't compromise." Especially not when it came to her beloved mountains.

"Good. Remember Lancaster's the priority. She's expendable."

The words, uttered between crackles and dead air, landed like rocks in his stomach. Will rallied against the reaction. Collateral damage had been part of every mission he'd accepted for his country. This wouldn't be any different.

Except he liked Charly and he wanted to know her better. Last night's dinner had started as a means to an end, but their previous dates had been a result of mutual attraction and friendship. And that kiss? He'd enjoyed it and, like any of his red-blooded male peers, it had left him working out how to get more.

More kisses and more of whatever she was willing to share beyond kisses.

"Lancaster is ruthless and…learned some things…he's out for blood," Casey said.

"Yes, sir." Will could fill in the missing words easily enough. "Let me know if you get anything on the beacon."

"It must…for the key…"

Will checked the display and moved again, hoping to hear a complete sentence this time. "…don't know how it got out there."

"I'll find it." He gave Casey the radio channels Binali Backcountry used and ended the call. Full of urgency, he navigated a route parallel to the track Charly was on and quickly closed the gap, catching up with them.

Despite the natural dangers, so far this assignment was a breeze. The mountain offered plenty of cover and resources. When he paused to listen or look around, the views were stunning.

But when he was in earshot of Lancaster again it was clear the older man wasn't as impressed with the environment. He became increasingly difficult for Charly as the day wore on, though she and Clint maintained their composure. Will watched the guides talk on two occasions, before and after lunch, and knew they were planning something. He didn't want to reveal himself or his purpose, but he couldn't let them jeopardize his mission, either. Casey and the authorities needed to know what had brought Lancaster out here, and Will couldn't let the guides jeopardize the primary objective.

As dinner wound down and Charly proposed setting up camp for the night, Lancaster protested again.

"There's plenty of light left," he shouted at her, sending birds that had roosted for the night winging into the air.

Will wasn't close enough to catch more than the sound of Charly's calm, quiet voice in reply. Taking a head count, grateful for the bright caps she gave to her guests, he planned his route and silently crept closer to the campsite.

"If we want to keep moving, you need to accommodate us," Lancaster said at a more reasonable volume. "Call the night hiking another team challenge," he added.

Clint spoke up. "That kind of challenge isn't worth the risk." He angled closer to Charly. "I have plenty of fun in store for tomorrow. It's better if we get some rest tonight."

"We're rested," Lancaster insisted.

The menacing tone, along with the eye contact between the others, had Will reaching for the knife in his boot. Could he break cover without causing more harm to people and the op?

He wasn't sure he had the leverage to ensure Lancaster's honest cooperation.

"There's a meteor shower this week," Charly said. "Tonight's peak time is only a few hours away."

"Not one of us gives a damn about the stars!"

"I know you want to reach the summit, and we'll get there," Charly was saying. Will admired her ability to stay calm despite the evidence that Lancaster wasn't here for the nature high. "Patience is important in these mountains. Especially at night. We're farther along than I'd planned, which makes tomorrow a shorter day."

"We go north." Lancaster's gaze roamed over each of his men in turn, and then he faced Charly once more. "Now."

"No." Charly, only two or three inches shorter than Lancaster, stared him down. "Night falls faster than you think and I won't risk it."

"We packed lights."

"No." She crossed her arms, feet planted.

"By your own rules—" Lancaster circled his finger, indicating his team. "We're in agreement."

"High risks or impromptu changes require a unanimous decision or a life-threatening circumstance." She tapped her chest. "I'm not hiking any more tonight."

"You misunderstand who is in charge here, Ms. Binali."

Her thick braid rippled between her shoulders as she shook her head. "Nature is in charge here, Mr. Lancaster," she shot back. "You can get mad or you can accept the facts. Darkness means predators and makes natural obstacles impossible to see. Flashlights aren't enough. My responsibility is to show you the mountain without injury or worse. That's why you hired me."

"I hired you to get me to the summit." He pulled out a heavy black handgun and leveled it on Charly. "The sooner the better."

Will braced for panic, but in the waning twilight Charly didn't flinch. "We stay here tonight."

"Whatever you're after, we'll find it tomorrow," Clint said.

Crap. Big mistake. Will wished he could do something, but he had to let Charly defuse this situation. Lancaster was too sure his target was north of here. Will would head that way, despite Charly's warning, just as soon as the group decided to stay put for the night.

Lancaster slowly turned to Clint, giving a nod to one of his men. "What do you know about it?"

"About what?" Clint tugged the bill of his ball cap. "I saw Max tracking something, that's all. I—"

The violent crack of gunfire ripped through the air and the forest seemed to shiver as wildlife reacted, scurrying through the shadows around Will.

Clint dropped to his knees, his hand clutched over the chest wound, blood oozing through his fingers, spreading across his shirt. Charly rushed to his side, doing her best to contain the bleeding, but Will knew it was a lost cause. A shot like that would've been fatal if they'd been standing fifty paces from a trauma center. Up here, in the middle of nowhere, Clint didn't stand a chance. In silent fury, helpless to intervene, Will swore as he watched the macabre scene unfold.

"Take the radios."

One of the men came forward and took the devices right off Charly and Clint. She was too focused on helping Clint to protest. Will couldn't blame her. Damn it. She'd be dead by morning at this rate. Mission protocol or not, he couldn't accept that. There had to be a way to get her out of here.

"Search the packs for a phone or anything else she might use against us." Lancaster barked out more orders about breaking camp before aiming his gun at Charly once more.

Will watched as her revolver, ammunition and flare gun were confiscated. Their cover blown, it didn't surprise him to see the operatives making their own weapons more accessible. He counted three rifles and each man moved a handgun into view. Two of them were left-handed. Those were just the weapons he could see—he had to assume there were more out of sight and plenty of ammunition to spare. A pretty big arsenal for a team of software engineers, but about right for mercenaries looking for a big payday.

"Get up." Lancaster gestured with his gun.

"I'm not leaving him."

Lancaster dropped to one knee, his voice low, the threat unmistakable. "I'm tired of you hindering me. I want your full cooperation." He tugged at her arm, but she wrenched away. "Get up. We're moving out right now."

"Go ahead and kill yourselves. I won't stop you. I'm staying with Clint."

Lancaster pushed to his feet, stalked a few paces away to talk with his men. The argument was loud and heated and centered around the tracking device Max carried. Even highly trained mercenaries had to sleep sometime. When they did, Will would make his move.

He ached for Charly, understanding how she felt. He'd lost teammates on operations and while he hadn't been there when it happened, he carried the burden of his younger brother in what was left of his heart.

She had to know Clint wouldn't survive, but she refused to give up on her friend. He respected the emotion fueling her determination, but he worried how she would cope when the adrenaline wore off and the grief set in.

She started to sing, rocking gently with Clint in her arms, and the strange words raised goose bumps on his arms. Clearly a song from her Native American heritage, the cadence and tune, the rise and fall of her voice felt older than time and completely in tune with the wilderness. Lancaster and his men stopped and stared as her voice rose, powered by her sorrow.

Will could even the odds right now, maybe take them all, but any miscalculation would put Charly in the crossfire. He dragged his attention back to the real problem: Lancaster. Only one thing would push the man this close to madness: Lancaster's revenge. Will felt certain the Blackout Key was somewhere on this mountain. It didn't matter if it made sense; he had to follow the most logical lead. Will could bide his time, take out Max and the tracking device, but he couldn't bring himself to leave Charly alone with this deadly crew.

If there was one thing Will managed on every op, it was getting creative when it mattered.

Chapter Seven

Clint was dying. In her arms. Charly felt him fading with every labored breath, every weak flutter of his heart. The copper scent of his blood choked the air.

A stronger woman would stand and fight, but that would leave Clint to die alone. She couldn't save him, but she wouldn't let him bleed out on the cold, unyielding mountain without any comfort.

Lancaster shouted at her, tugged at her, but she didn't listen. One of his men seized the radios and their packs. None of that mattered. Her hand pressed to her friend's wound, she tried desperately to slow the bleeding. Despite the losing battle, she put on a brave face. "It's not that bad," she murmured. "You'll make it."

"Right." He looked at her out of glassy eyes, his lips twitching in an effort to grin. "Could be worse."

She understood the sentiment even as her

heart clutched with agony. In their line of work, accidents were inevitable, natural disasters a daily risk. Safety precautions failed. Between her friends and family, they often discussed there were worse ways to die than under a big sky in nature's embrace, doing what they loved.

"You'll make it," she repeated.

His head jerked to the side and his breath stuttered. "Get away."

"Together," she insisted. His eyelids drifted shut and she willed them to open one more time. It was too soon for goodbye. "Clint." She gave him a little shake with her trembling arms. "Hang on. We'll find help."

She rambled more nonsense as her elders' chants of sorrow whispered through her mind, echoed through the trees. Words and prayers that should be spoken for Clint, over him, and she was the only one to speak them. If she couldn't save her friend, at least she could honor him.

The words were soft at first, but her voice gained strength as Clint's life drained away. She let the songs and the spirit behind them flow over him like a gentle rain. Tipping her face to the clear night sky, the soft breeze dried her tears as she called on the heritage beating through her heart to guide and protect Clint on his next journey.

She finished the prayer, let the final note

drift into the coming night. Opening her eyes, she looked down at her bloodstained hands, at Clint's lifeless body, and felt gravity dragging her down.

"Move out."

Lancaster's voice was hard and ugly and Charly ignored him. Her work wasn't done. She walked toward the shallow creek and knelt down, washing the blood from her hands.

"We're moving out." Lancaster hauled her to her feet.

"Good luck to you." She wouldn't waste energy hurling fury at him. She would not taint the grace of the moment or the task ahead by slinging insults and venom at the man who stole Clint's life. There would be time for that later. "I must bury my friend."

"A futile, sentimental gesture."

Her body coiled to strike, to lash out, but it would be a useless gesture and prevent her from completing a necessary task. "Clint deserves better than to have animals tearing at his body." She picked up a stone only to have Lancaster knock it from her hands. She picked it up again, imagining herself in a Teflon bubble, his anger sliding off her as he followed her back to the body.

"Have you ever seen what scavengers can do?" she asked no one in particular. "You wouldn't wish it on your worst enemy." Back and forth, she hauled stones one by one to cover Clint.

"On top of that," she continued in her educational tone, "all the blood will attract predators. Are you prepared to outmaneuver them?"

Around her the men argued, uncertain how to proceed. Lancaster wanted to keep moving, others wanted to wait. All of them thought she'd lost her mind, but they were divided about the wisdom of leaving her behind. In a tiny corner of her mind Charly listened, amused, while her body kept on task.

"Pick up your pack or I'll shoot you, too," Lancaster threatened, his gun aimed at her face, when she'd placed yet another stone on Clint's incomplete grave.

"Go ahead." She turned her back on him, refusing to cow to his bluster and bullying. "You and your gadgets will have all kinds of fun up here without me."

More arguing was silenced by a wolf howl slicing through the night.

"Scavengers," she said.

"There are wolves out here?"

She didn't stop moving, but she slid a look at Jeff, the man who'd asked the question. "Didn't you listen at all? There are wolves, snakes, mountain lions, bears—"

"Shut up!" Lancaster bellowed.

With a shrug, she continued her work, not surprised Jeff joined her.

"What the hell are you doing?" Scott demanded, blocking Jeff's attempt to help her bury Clint.

"The sooner we get this done, the sooner we get out of here."

"Thank you," Charly said. "Clint wouldn't approve of being an easy meal."

Her back ached; her hands were cold and bleeding with fresh scrapes on her knuckles and palms. The sting felt good, reminding her she was alive and doing the right thing. Not just for Clint, but to defy Lancaster.

Knowing it made them uncomfortable, she started to sing again, the old creation story-song her grandmother had taught her. It had been one of Clint's favorites. Charly decided she would sing all of the songs of her childhood to honor Clint and keep Lancaster and his men on edge.

No one usually cared that she was part of the Ute nation. Her clients typically only asked about her Native American lineage when she led them down into the pueblos and canyons. Why couldn't Lancaster have headed that direction? The pueblos were riddled with places to lose these guys. Even better, that area was littered with ways to scare them to death and even up the long odds against her. That would've been fun.

It would take cleverness and a good share of luck to escape all seven men up here. On this part of the ridge, there were thick stands of trees, but also wide-open places. They were armed, but she had the real advantage. She knew her way over every inch of wild land east of the Four Corners Monument all the way to Telluride. She knew what the mountain offered by way of protection and danger. If she could be patient, she could clip them off one at a time, like a wolf culling a buffalo herd.

The image made her smile.

"What are you so happy about?" Lancaster had stepped into her path once more. "Your friend is dead and you'll join him when I'm done with you."

She looked straight into his eyes and thought she saw the glare of madness, something he'd hidden well when he hired her yesterday. "It would be an honor to join my friend. There are worse ways to die than out here under the big sky."

"You're crazy."

Possibly. Right now she didn't care if he shot her and she sure as hell didn't care about his opinion of her sanity. With a shrug, she stepped around him, determined to finish the burial. "Takes one to know one," she said, resuming her story-song.

Rich joined Jeff's efforts, and she couldn't get angry about their help. Soon Clint's body and the bloodstained earth around it were covered. The rocks glowed pale in the light of the rising moon.

One of Lancaster's men had started a fire, effectively ending the discussion of moving on tonight. If she'd known which man, she might've thanked him. Exhaustion crept up on her, and her limbs felt heavy as she rested near Clint's grave. But though her eyelids drooped, she listened to the talk of the men around her. They weren't careless enough to reveal the specifics, but whatever beacon they were following appeared to be on the other side of the peak.

She fought the urge to laugh. Assuming the beacon's signal wasn't distorted by the mountains, Lancaster and his men would soon discover just how much wide-open space they would have to cross to reach their goal.

She didn't argue when it was decided she'd spend the night tied to a tree away from the fire, away from Clint. She didn't care that Jeff would take the first watch as her guard.

Lancaster allowed her the use of her sleeping bag and a bottle of water only so she'd be more useful tomorrow. Jeff found the small knife she kept in her boot when he tethered her to the tree with nylon rope, but he didn't raise the alarm, merely pocketed it without a word.

In her anguished haze she felt some remorse that she'd have to hurt the one man in this crew with a shred of decency, but it had to be done. She would not be here when Lancaster woke in the morning.

WILL LISTENED TO the men argue as Charly slowly buried Clint. Unsure how much of the conversation she heard, he marveled at her unwavering behavior in the face of their cold discussion about killing her.

He'd certainly never seen anyone as resolute in a task as Charly hauling rocks to cover Clint's body. Hopefully it wasn't a sign that she'd snapped. Even if it was, he'd get her off this mountain in one piece so she could recover with people who loved her.

When Will was convinced Lancaster wouldn't shoot her out of temper or spite, he backed away from the camp, moving through the shadows until he couldn't hear her haunting voice any longer.

At the edge of a tree line, he paused and gathered himself before he even attempted to make the call to Casey. He'd seen men die. He'd been responsible for putting more than a few bad guys out of commission. But never had he witnessed anything as beautiful as the tribute Charly paid Clint.

The memory of his brother's funeral slammed to the front of Will's mind. He didn't want to go there, had more than enough to deal with, yet he knew better than to fight the onslaught. When those memories were triggered, they faded faster if he simply let them flow.

The chapel had been standing room only, the casket closed. He'd walked forward to join the family—his parents—only to realize too late that there wasn't a seat for him. His mother had lifted her blotchy, tearstained face and stared at him with so much blame the words weren't necessary.

After so many times rehashing and reliving that terrible moment, Will expected the bitterness and ache to fade, but it remained fresh and raw.

He'd never heard anything as haunting as Charly's voice raised in that strange benediction. At first he'd thought it was grief, but he'd seen plenty of that along the way. Her song or prayer or whatever it was had clearly been offered as tribute for Clint.

He knew it was natural in the wake of death to think about his mortality. Will knew no one would ever grieve that way for him. He couldn't dwell on it because it was part of the job. As a SEAL he'd accepted the possibility of dying anonymously in the line of duty. He considered it an honor.

Pulling in a deep breath of the cold night air, he steeled himself for the work ahead. Nothing had changed except the number of innocents in the equation. He checked the signal on his phone and despite the miniscule single bar, he dialed Casey's office.

As the phone rang on the other end of the line, Will resolved that when they got off this mountain he would have Charly tell him about her song for Clint. It always helped him to have an end goal on a mission, especially a mission with long odds and high stakes. One against seven could almost be fun, as long as Charly came through unscathed.

The director answered, and Will snapped to full alert.

The signal was remarkably clear this time. "Lancaster shot one guide. The crew is camped for the night, but determined to reach the summit and points north ASAP."

"Still following a beacon?" Casey asked.

"Yes, sir. Could he have put it on the key somehow?"

"That's my fear. We've connected a few dots. Lancaster didn't disappear until a plane he was expecting to meet in Los Angeles never showed up. It's possible the software, or someone transporting it was on the plane, but I don't have any names to work with yet."

"I haven't heard any news of a plane crash around here," Will replied. Surely that kind of thing would've caught someone's attention.

"We know it was a small private charter. If it was off course or skirting radar systems, no one would know."

True. Calling in a helicopter to search for a missing plane was out of the question. Up here, in the thin air, there had to be a starting point and a reason to justify the risk. Neither was available with the limited intel. The altitude and terrain would cause all sorts of problems for both plane and helo pilots.

Will felt the weight of the world drop onto his shoulders. He and Charly—and a mountain— were the only things standing between Lancaster and whatever he had planned.

"Everything in the Los Angeles office and home point to a revenge strike against the big developers," Casey said. "After his long silence he wasn't even trying to hide his hate and vengeance anymore."

"Which means he's all or nothing out here." *Great.* Will sighed, rubbing the knots of tension at the base of his neck.

"Exactly," Casey agreed. "If the software was on that plane, he'll do anything to reach it."

"Could the key even survive the crash?"

"Lancaster must believe it has."

"He's a man with focus, that's for sure," Will allowed. Men like that were a crazy kind of dangerous.

"Can you get to the crash site before Lancaster's team?"

It didn't sound as though he had much of a choice. "Without set coordinates, I doubt it. But I can definitely keep them from leaving with the key if it's there."

"That's the objective. You're all that's standing between a madman and every locked door in the nation. Hell, the world. The intel coming in paints an ugly picture, Will."

Will thought it couldn't be much uglier than what he'd been watching unfold a few klicks away. "I can eliminate him and seize the tracker." It would be the clean, fast resolution. Then Casey could bring in experts to secure the plane and the key.

The silence stretched so long Will thought the call had dropped. "No," Casey said. "We need him alive. He's the only person who knows how to deconstruct the Blackout Key. He's likely the only one who can code a counter response if the key gets out into the world."

Will didn't offer his opinion that Lancaster wouldn't cooperate with authorities. Casey had to know that already and Will got paid for action, not opinions. If they needed Lancaster alive, Will would take him alive. It would be easier if he had a better read on the crew surrounding Lancaster. Would they bail if their boss fell apart, or were they dedicated to the madman's cause? "Do you have any intel on the mercenaries with him? Are they here for a big payout or something else?"

"No idea. We're combing his life for clues. What have you observed?"

Nothing new, Will thought. "Ruthless. Arms are US made." Which didn't clarify anything. American guns and ammunition remained a hot commodity and could be attained legally or otherwise from just about anywhere in the world. The men were also freaked out by Charly's behavior, but he didn't add that. "I'm fairly confident they're American."

"Stay on it. More information could lead to the second-tier targets after Lancaster's vendetta is satisfied."

"Stay tuned to the emergency radio channels." He'd said it before, but it bore repeating. Most people didn't understand the limited communication in these mountains. Worried about Charly, Will wanted to get back over to the camp. "Up here it may be my only way for me to get information out."

"All right."

Hearing Casey's frustration, Will sympathized. "Lancaster thinks he's close. I'll be there when he finds it."

"Good luck."

Will powered off the phone and returned it to his pocket. He wouldn't risk it again for hours and wanted to preserve the battery. While he had a solar-powered backup battery with him, he didn't anticipate having the luxury of recharging time.

His mind working, he carefully picked his way back toward the camp, slowing as he got closer and listening for sentries.

He heard the wilderness—the hoot of an owl and the rustle of small prey in the underbrush—but he didn't hear any sound of humans. When he caught the smoky scent of the banked fire, he followed his instincts and crossed the stream.

It was unlikely anyone posted to keep watch would bother with more than a cursory glance in this direction. They'd consider the stream a natural barrier to predators of any variety. Lancaster's men weren't expecting any company out here anyway.

Will hunkered down at the base of a tree and waited for some sign of a sentry. He let half an hour tick by and with no sign or sound, he crept closer. The arrogance of men had made his job easier in the past and he never turned down a gimme when it fell into his lap.

Staying on the far side of the little stream, Will did a head count. Twice. Coming up one short, he circled the camp and counted again. Seven people. Six prone, resting close to the fire, and all of them a safe distance from Clint's rocky grave. All of them were breathing. One man sat apart from the others, leaning upright against a tree. Next to an empty sleeping bag.

Where had they put Charly?

His pulse raced and he felt the hot lick of panic for the first time since his early training days when the physical tests had pushed his body to the red zone. He forced himself away from illogical, unproven assumptions. Lancaster's men had refused to continue without her guidance. That ripple of dissent hadn't made Lancaster happy, but it was the reason Will had retreated to give his update.

Will counted one more time. Seven men. Zero women.

Charly wasn't in the camp.

Had Lancaster snapped and killed her anyway? No, if Lancaster had done that the men would've moved on as he'd wanted all along. He moved closer to the seated man. Close enough to notice the man's hands were tied, to see the thin line of drying blood at his throat.

Will thought of the knife Charly had tucked into her sleeping bag and breathed a quiet sigh. The rush of relief was a palpable force.

Now he just had to find her. An expert tracker in a cold forest shrouded by night. He'd wanted a challenge.

Chapter Eight

An hour earlier

Charly's heart pounded in her ribs as she shifted in her sleeping bag, trying to get comfortable while being tied to the tree behind Jeff. He'd done it up right, looping the rope around her ankle, then around the tree and pinning it with a tent stake. Leaning back against the tree trunk, he'd made a point of adding his key chain to the assembly, so even if he dozed off, he'd hear the rattle if she tried to escape.

Too bad for him that wasn't going to stop her. She stared sightlessly at Clint's grave, waiting for the other men to stop bickering and settle down. It took only a little less than an eternity. She rolled to her other side, kicking her legs a little and rattling the key against the tent stake. Jeff looked her way, but no one else said a word.

She needed to get out of here, and she would. But it would be foolish to bolt into the night with no plan. As she tossed and turned in her sleeping bag, she reviewed her choices and Lancaster's potential reactions to each.

Instinct warred with reality. Rushing straight back to Durango sounded ideal, but Lancaster could easily head off that kind of play. She knew the terrain, but he had the radios and rifles. If she aimed west for the nearest park ranger station, she had a better chance. While no one could track like her, she'd seen enough to know Lancaster's men weren't idiots. The crucial element, she decided, was getting away clean. Tonight was her best chance. Tomorrow he might kill her for any number of reasons.

She peered at her guard through slitted eyes and found him alert, scanning the area. So he took the watch responsibilities seriously. Sucker.

When she was a teenager, and even before that, when she'd started solo hikes, her family had taught her how to be safe up here. How to read animal tracks and watch for shifting weather. The wilderness was beauty and magnificence honed to a sharp and dangerous edge. She'd learned a little something from everyone in her family about protecting and defending herself from nature and man.

The sleeve sewn under the pillow of her sleeping bag had been a precaution against drunk or stupid hikers who might get the wrong idea about the services Binali Backcountry provided on overnight adventures. It was a rare thing, praise God, to fend off unwelcome advances, but it was better to be prepared than caught unawares. She counted it lucky that she'd chosen to tuck the knife from her grandmother into her sleeping bag this time out. It calmed her down and gave her a sense of empowerment as her fingers rubbed the familiar turquoise inlay.

Confident the other men were settled and asleep, she curled onto her side, jerking the tether on purpose again and adding a sniffle for effect.

"Go to sleep," Jeff said, keeping his voice low.

"I'm trying to get my boots off," she lied.

"Keep them on. Your feet will get cold."

"How nice of you to care," she muttered. "Feet and boots need to air out to stay healthy."

"Whatever." He shifted, adjusting his back against the tree. "Sleep."

"You know I'm right. I hope you packed lots of socks. For a guy with obvious field training, you're ignoring the basics."

"Quiet," he snapped. A moment later, she gave a mental cheer as he unlaced his boots.

It was a start. "You'll never get away with this," she said after a few more minutes.

"Our plans are not your problem, Ms. Binali."

She rattled the tether. "I beg to differ."

"Shut up."

She didn't stop rattling the key against the tent stake, even as the knife slid through the rope, freeing her. She wanted him to come at her, to give her a better reason than escape to sink her blade between his ribs.

Charly wouldn't relish killing a man, but she knew she could do it if necessary. Jeff might not have pulled the trigger, but he was part of something dark and evil by staying loyal to Lancaster.

Of course, Jeff had been the first to show compassion by helping her bury her friend. She preferred a solution for him that didn't involve death.

Survival was paramount. Her survival. Whatever these men were up to, when she escaped she trusted the mountain to keep them busy or kill them off until she could return with the authorities. Either by nature's law or man's law, one way or another Lancaster and his men would pay for murdering Clint.

"Stop screwing around," Jeff said, his impatience clear. "I can make this worse for you."

"I'd like to see you try," she dared. She'd considered the various ploys to get him to come closer. Seduction was out—even if she could stomach the idea long enough to get away, she didn't think Jeff or any of the others would fall for it.

She'd sensed a shift among them when she'd refused to quake and cower at the wrong end of Lancaster's gun. She'd sensed their fear. Not just of Lancaster's actions, but of her. On some level her reactions and her tribute to Clint scared them. With Jeff in particular, she would use that fear and spare his life. If possible.

She stared him down as she rolled over once more and rattled the key.

"Enough." He pushed to his feet, the scowl on his face twisting his features in the eerie glow from the fire.

She tucked the knife away and stood up as well, keeping her boots and the severed nylon rope covered by the folds of her sleeping bag. "Give me your hands," he ordered, pitching his voice low.

She held them out and used the distraction to block the knee she aimed at his groin. He buckled forward on a whimper and she drove her fist up deep into his diaphragm.

Pivoting him as he collapsed, she let him slide down the trunk of the tree until he was back where he started. He stared up at her with wide eyes full of shock and pain, unable to voice a protest as she retrieved her gun and ammunition. She tossed the radio out of reach.

She pressed her knife to Jeff's throat. "I could kill you."

He froze, his eyes locked with hers, though she could tell he wanted to keep rocking against the pain.

She drew the blade against his skin, just a scratch, but it raised a narrow line of blood. It distracted him from her real purpose, which was putting him into a deep sleep. When she found the pressure point in his neck, he went limp and she quickly tied his hands.

Unwilling to waste time and risk waking the others, Charly didn't take so much as a canteen as she darted, silent as an owl, into the dark. She knew how to survive off the mountain. Conveniently bottled water and packaged food would be more burden than help to her.

She started straight down the mountain, aiming for the nearest official trail, leaving a heavy boot print every few paces. She dropped her company ball cap at one point and veered sharply away, scuffing at the dirt as if she'd paused in the shelter of a tree to get her bearings. If she'd drawn a map for Lancaster it wouldn't have been as clear. If she was lucky, his arrogance and low opinion of her would be enough to follow this trail without question.

Right into her trap.

With no idea how much of a head start she had, she moved quickly, hoping the screen would hold up in the light of day. Maybe they'd search for her early and follow her tracks right over the edge of this rock slide and into the stream below. At least one of them would be injured, hopefully more, and that would start to even the odds.

As she finished, she willed her heart to be quiet so she could hear any pursuit. Hearing no sign of Lancaster's men, she moved on, this time without a trace. Every step of freedom was a pure joy, despite the heavy burden of Clint's death. The *should have done*s nipped at her conscience, telling her Clint might be alive if she'd handled things differently.

It was bull, she told herself, a natural result of being alive. Caving to guilt and fear and regret would only get her caught and killed. The best hope, the only real option, was to reach a ranger station and make a full report. Preferably by dawn.

Her mind set, she crept closer toward her real goal, picking her way through the fractured shadows of the forest. She'd only gone a few paces in that direction when she heard the distinct snap of a twig. She slowly turned toward the sound, straining to hear something that would give her a clue as to what was out there.

But the forest had gone still along with her. Not a good sign—that kind of stillness indicated something was out here that shouldn't be. Knowing exactly where she was, she knew she was too far from any real safety. Damn it. She'd never expected any of Lancaster's men to be this good.

They'd been heavy-footed and generally dismissive of their surroundings all day, making plenty of noise on the hike. Had it been an act?

Well, with any luck there'd be time and breath to berate herself later. Calculating the risk, she charged toward the break in the tree line. Her breath sawed in and out of her lungs as she pumped her arms and legs, plowing forward. Being exposed in the open space wouldn't be ideal, but she could minimize that in a race for the drop on the opposite side.

Almost there, close enough to see the moonlight on the high meadow, she went down hard under a heavy mass. She rolled with the tackle, kicking her legs out and pushing her assailant away.

On a grunted oath, she realized this wasn't something as simple as a confused bear or curious mountain lion. She wasn't that lucky. This was a man bent on subduing her. He lunged again, trapping her legs in a brutal grip against his chest.

Hell, no.

She wasn't going back to Lancaster, wasn't going down like this. Ignoring the bite of various bits of nature on the forest floor, she squirmed and rolled until he was on top of her. She drove her elbows into the sensitive points at the top of his shoulders, trying to get enough space to draw the gun or knife.

The reflexive release was short-lived. The grip loosened only enough so he could shift higher, wrapping her tightly and pinning her arms to her sides.

"It's me. Will."

The voice, hoarse in her ear, was foreign to her. She fought to get a leg free to strike, but his legs were stronger still.

"Relax, Charly."

As if. It had to be a trick. Will was in town. She let her body go limp, pretending to comply. When the man eased up, she scooped a handful of dirt and dried leaves into his face.

His muffled oath followed her across the moonlight-soaked meadow. She didn't look back—didn't have to, she could hear him closing in fast. His hands caught in her jacket, slowing her down. She shrugged out of it and shot ahead.

"Charly!"

Aiming straight for the drop-off, knowing the cost of her survival would involve plenty of pain, she kept going.

But he caught her again, slowing her just enough that they went over the edge together. As her body bounced down the rocky slope, knocking the air from her lungs, bright spots of light danced across her vision.

They skidded to a stop, and she willed herself to fight on, but her body wouldn't cooperate.

"Charly! Wake up. I'm here to help."

Hearing Will's voice she knew she was either dead or hallucinating. Will couldn't be here. He was down in Durango delivering mail. Waiting at the pub for another game of pool. She batted away the hands sweeping over her face, smoothing her hair.

"That's my girl. You're safe now."

It was a challenge to muster the energy to open her eyes. Her brain was playing tricks on her. Will couldn't be here. And she didn't care about cooperating in the slightest way with any of Lancaster's men.

"Just shoot me and call it done," she mumbled, feeling defeated. She couldn't beat them.

"No way. I'm not done with you."

The man who sounded like Will kissed her forehead. The touch was offensive and her melting reaction to it was worse. She rallied in outrage. Shoving the man off her, she scooted out of reach.

"Back off." She jerked the knife from her boot, holding it ready though she couldn't quite see her attacker in the weak light of the moon.

"Take it easy, Charly. Put that away."

She blinked several times to clear her vision. She must've taken a hard blow to the head. In the moonlight, this guy actually looked like Will. "This is a nightmare. You're a bad dream."

"It's good to see you, too," he said with a little laugh.

She knew that sound, that laugh. This was a serious hallucination. She rubbed her eyes with one hand, knife clutched in the other. "You can't be...can't be here." She pressed her fingers against the ache building in her temples. "You're in Durango."

"Not anymore. You're safe now. Put the knife away."

As her eyes adjusted and his features became clearer, she did as he asked and sheathed the knife. "It's really you."

"Yes." His mouth tilted in that lopsided smile she liked. "I'm here to help."

"What?" What did that mean? This was a sick dream. She had to wake up, had to reach the ranger station. Determined, she tried to stand, called it a good start when she managed to stay upright a few seconds before slumping against the nearest boulder. Her ribs ached and her hands were stinging with fresh scrapes.

"Have some water."

She eyed the bottle he held out. "You first." He twisted off the top and tipped it back. "Fine," she said, accepting. She sniffed at it and then took a long drink, letting it slide down and soothe her dry throat.

"Believe it's me yet?"

"Maybe by daylight," she replied, shivering.

"I have a flashlight."

"I have a gun," she countered, wondering if it was still true. "Don't bother with the light." It could draw the others.

"You sound steadier."

"Yay," she said through chattering teeth.

"I'm here for you, Charly. Tell me how to help."

"Who the hell *are* you?"

"It's me, Will Chase. Were you expecting someone else?"

Yeah, she was expecting Jeff or one of the others. She still expected one or all of them to burst out of the night and attack. "You're working for them."

"Absolutely not. I'm on your side. You have to believe that."

She did. On instinct, she did believe him. Though she didn't understand how it was possible for him to be here. Maybe this was one of those spirit guide dreams. She nearly laughed, thinking how absurd it would be if her spirit guide was a white mailman from Illinois.

"Charly, sit down here beside me."

"We're not safe here."

"Sure we are."

She shook her head, wobbling a bit. "Did you drug me?"

"No, but my guess is you're a little dazed. Possibly dealing with mild shock."

"That's impossible." She couldn't be dazed or in shock. No time for that nonsense. Shivering, she didn't protest when he put her back into her polar fleece coat and wrapped an arm around her waist. She felt the weight of her revolver in her pocket. If he was with the bad guys, he wouldn't let her keep her weapons. He guided her under the shelter of an overhang and helped her sit down. "You've been through hell the past few hours," he said in that easy way he had.

It felt better to sit down, her legs outstretched, Will's hard body warm beside her. She didn't know how he'd found her and she needed a few answers, but she understood she was crashing from the stress of a sustained fight-or-flight response.

Her body recognized him even if her mind argued obstinately. Relaxing into his embrace, she let her head drop to his shoulder. "Clint is dead," she whispered into the night.

"I know, baby."

"He's dead." She looked down at her hands,

muted smears against her khaki hiking pants. "He died in my arms."

"I know."

WILL BREATHED EASIER when Charly fell asleep. Giving her time to rest was the least he could do after the wicked fight she'd put up. If he'd known giving away his position would result in her rushing headlong off the mountainside, he would've come up with a better way to let her know he was there.

Her lean body was solid muscle under those subtle, feminine curves.

When he'd found the gun in her jacket, he counted himself lucky she hadn't shot him. He'd expected the knife—it only made sense—but she hadn't used either against him. He chalked it up to her being in full-flight mode. She'd done everything—including run off a small cliff—to get away from him.

It hadn't been easy to find her in the dark; if she hadn't left that bogus trail before doubling back, he might still be wandering around. The woman could move with the absolute silence and grace of a mountain lion when she chose. It had been more than a little spooky to watch her.

She didn't make a sound or leave a trace unless she wanted to, although their wrestling match on the other side of the meadow had left plenty of evidence that would gather unwelcome attention if Lancaster bothered to search this far.

It wouldn't matter. The only way Will could be sure what Reed Lancaster was up to was to stay on the man's tail. He smoothed a hand over the silk of Charly's midnight hair, hoping when she woke up she'd be willing to help him execute his plan. If they found the plane or key Lancaster was searching for, they could put this mission to bed and she could get back to her regularly scheduled life.

Chapter Nine

Hours later, under the weak light of a dawn shrouded by misty rain, Charly planted her hands on her hips and glared daggers at Will. "We're not going back to where those devils are." She shook her head. "Absolutely not." Her muscles ached, her eyes felt gritty. Every time she looked at her hands she saw Clint's blood. She wasn't going to take any chances that Lancaster would escape justice. They needed the authorities up here. "We have to go for help."

"I am the help," Will said.

She wanted to believe it. Admittedly, he'd helped her last night, giving her shelter and security to recover a bit. "Why didn't you announce yourself rather than chase me?"

"I let you know I was there."

"Breaking a twig hardly counts." She needed to get over it, but it annoyed her that she hadn't even sensed him until he'd taken action. Mailmen weren't typically praised for stealth.

"You're pissed thinking I got the better of you, but really it was sheer luck I caught you before you disappeared from the false trail you laid."

She pushed her hands through her hair, combing out the tangles and wishing she hadn't ditched her ball cap in that effort. "How can we be sure you didn't leave signs out there showing them exactly where to find me?"

"They aren't here, are they?"

Fair point. She blew her hair away from her face.

"What do you need from me, Charly?"

His tone was as hard as the grim look on his face. She'd never seen him so serious. It scared her a little. Resigned, she pulled her hair forward over her shoulder and started weaving it into a braid. She didn't miss the way his eyes tracked the motions.

"Nothing," she insisted. "I'm going up to the ranger station to let them know Lancaster is a problem child. You go ahead and do whatever you have to do."

He'd told her he was on some kind of undercover assignment, but she couldn't quite wrap her head around that yet. Not that he hadn't proven himself capable—last night's fight was plenty of evidence. Could her mailman really be *this* guy?

They'd gone out a few times, but she wasn't

naive enough to think he owed her anything. What irked her was how he'd given her a taste of the facts without telling her anything of real value. Navy was one thing. SEAL was completely different.

"I don't want you out here alone," he argued, not for the first time since he'd woken her.

"I can handle myself."

"In any other situation I'd agree."

Charly stamped her feet and blew into her cupped palms. It would be cold most of the day. The overhang offered a break from the worst bite of the wind, but a fire would've been nice. They just couldn't risk it.

"Aren't you going to say anything?"

Charly stared at Will. There was no mistaking the honesty in his clear blue eyes. How could she have been so wrong about a person? Her mailman, her new friend, the guy she'd wanted to be more…well, based on the story he'd told her, he sure was more.

"Undercover?" She echoed the word he'd used when he'd tried to explain.

Will nodded. "I didn't expect anything to happen this soon. If ever."

"Unexpected is part of it, right?"

Again, the nod.

She couldn't figure out why her feelings were hurt. He hadn't led her on or used her, but she still felt cheated. Deceived. "Was I some kind of target?"

"No." He reached out, then let his hands drop. "Before Lancaster, no one in Durango was a target. You have a reputation for tracking, but that's not why I asked you out." His gaze roamed past her shoulder and over the horizon, then returned to her, but he didn't elaborate. "We don't really have time to do this now," he said flatly.

She supposed he would know more about the timeline for managing this problem than she did. "You're convinced Lancaster's trying to reach a crashed plane?"

According to Will, her deceptive client was out here trying to recover a bit of technology for his master plan. A plan that could break through any kind of security encryption. She thought about the vast size of the forest. The needle-in-a-haystack image didn't come close.

"That's how the intel is shaping up."

Undercover mailman. Government intel. A dead friend. She chewed on her lip. It was a lot to take in. He'd told her being a mailman in Durango went with the assignment. A *mailman*. She gave whoever had dreamed that up points for originality. Undercover explained the extreme fitness, and he'd certainly proved himself skilled and capable out here. It added up… but her *mailman*?

How had she let herself be so blinded? Tammy's voice popped into her head. Will had plenty of "blinding" features. The shoulders. The ass. Couldn't forget the eyes. Or the sexy scar on his chin.

"How'd you get the scar?"

He swiped at the thin white line with his fingers, then stuffed his hands into his pockets. "I'll tell you on the way back to Lancaster's camp."

Charly planted her hands on her hips and glared daggers at him. "Tell me on the way to the ranger station." She wasn't ready to go back. She might never be ready to face Lancaster again. The idea made her stomach clench. No matter how much she scrubbed, she knew she'd see Clint's blood on her hands for days. Longer. They were going back to Durango and alerting the authorities. She would not entertain any ideas that allowed Lancaster to escape justice.

"I have to stay on Lancaster," Will said softly.

She believed him, knew he'd probably spent more time than he should have caring for her overnight.

"I could use your expertise."

She didn't like that he knew just which buttons to push. She didn't want to part ways, didn't want to evaluate all of her reasons. "If you need to go back, fine. I'll get back to town and file a formal report against Lancaster for murder. That should make your job easier."

"That's not smart." His breath made soft clouds in the cold air. "We need to stick together on this."

She shook her head. Tracking was one thing. Tracking seven armed men, one of them too ready to kill—no. "We're both adults here. I can take care of myself.

"I don't want you out here alone," he said again. "He'll send someone for you."

"And I'll be ready." She patted the gun in her jacket pocket. "Don't worry about me. I'll be fine."

He grumbled something she couldn't quite make out. Wasn't sure she wanted to hear. She didn't ask because she was done wasting daylight. "Well." She knelt down to adjust the laces on her boots, struggling to keep herself together. "Thanks for the assist last night."

"What if we go straight for the plane?"

"I beg your pardon?" The idea was absurd.

He crouched beside her. "We know where he's going, so we beat him to the prize."

She stood up and paced away as Will kept talking.

"Sending men after you means better numbers for us. Two against six, then hopefully just five."

"If we take his prize, as you put it, he'll come after us."

"Exactly. Giving us the power to lead him wherever we want him to end up."

The idea had merit. It appealed to the voice in her heart clamoring to avenge Clint. But two against five, probably six? "One problem."

"Only one? That's doable."

She fought off her amusement at his bald confidence. "We don't know where the plane is."

"Sure we do."

"More intel?"

"Yes." He stepped close to her. "Your intel."

His fingertips brushed her temple, and she locked her knees to keep them steady. The heat of his body, so close, tempted her on a level that had nothing to do with national security. Different scenarios played through her head. Getting caught by Lancaster's men. Running off with Will. Lancaster getting away with murder. Will might only have one problem, but suddenly she felt inundated.

She focused on the biggest one first. Going after the plane was akin to snipe hunting. There were too many places it could be. Even more likely, pieces of wreckage could be scattered across miles. "Why do you think I have any information?"

"You're the best tracker in four states, Charly."

He delivered the statement with such sincerity. Not helpful. She gave a snort, tried to create a little distance, but he wouldn't give her an inch. "In order to track something, tracks are required."

His hands cruised gently over her shoulders. She wanted to lean in, to believe that something they'd shared in Durango had been more than his job. She resisted.

"He argued with you about the route, right?"

"Yes." She looked up into his eyes. "You were following us a long time." Close enough to listen in, and she hadn't known. She was glad Will played for America and not against.

He shrugged. "Off and on from the start." He stepped back, catching her hand with his, drawing her along with him.

From the start. She wrenched free of him. "You interrogated me last night."

He jerked back as if she'd hit him. "I did no such thing."

She waved her hands. "The night before. Over burgers and milkshakes, you interrogated me."

"That's stretching the definition."

"Is it? You asked me routes and times and—" She felt the heat flood her face with the embarrassment of it all. He'd kissed her goodbye. Their first real kiss hadn't been real at all. "You kissed me!"

"You didn't complain at the time."

She clamped her lips shut, covered them with a hand to keep from cursing him. Not that she really believed the wind would snatch him away on her command, but why take the chance? "You didn't give me so much as a warning!" She wanted to shout, but knew better than to indulge her temper that way. If by some horrible stroke of luck Lancaster's men were on the right trail, she wouldn't be responsible for making it easier for them.

"What was I supposed to tell you?" He leaned back against the rock wall, hands in his pockets, his dark blue gaze unrelenting. "Any warning I might have given you required a long explanation I wasn't cleared to give. There are restrictions that go along with my job."

No job was worth Clint's life. The fresh wave of sorrow stole her breath. "You thought it was better to send me up the mountain with a pack of wolves in engineers' clothing?"

"Yes." He tilted his head and cracked his neck.

"Clint died."

He didn't shy away from her blatant accusation. "You'd both be dead if I'd warned you."

She wanted to be angry; instead it seemed all she could muster was more misery and grief. She'd lost a friend. Two, counting Will.

"Warning you would've caused more problems," he contended.

"I wouldn't have brought him up here," she countered.

Will shook his head. "If you'd accepted my warning and *if* you'd believed my story, I think you would've gone ahead with this hike. But with my warning in your head, suspecting Lancaster was a problem waiting to happen would've made you nervous. He would've acted sooner and taken his chances on his own."

"You don't know that."

"He's desperate, Charly." His quiet voice, full of sympathy, pricked her conscience. "You've seen that for yourself."

Her arms were suddenly heavy as she remembered Clint's lifeless body. She wanted to look away from Will, wanted to deny the logic in his explanation. Instead, she faced him head-on. "Were you out there?"

"Yes."

She gave him points for not pretending to misunderstand the question. "You didn't do anything."

"I did what I thought best to protect you."

What did that mean? Her mind spun. She'd been a fool to think a man like her ripped, smart mailman could really be into her. "I thought you were interested in me."

"I am."

Unbelievable. In fact, she believed everything he said but that. She rolled her eyes. "God, I'm gullible. You—" she waved her hands, indicating his whole body "—interested in me," she repeated, incredulous. "I started to care."

There it was—her real sticking point. She'd started to care for him, *about* him. She'd started to let the romantic fantasy color her view, making her see his actions and reactions in ways he didn't intend. "Wow," she muttered, owning her weakness. "That must've put you in a tight spot."

"No." He took a step toward her. "Charly, hear me out."

She held up a hand, silencing him. She didn't want to hear any more about how she'd developed a crush on the hot guy with the job to do. "Only if it's about the plane. If I can help you with that, fine, but please don't make me rehash the other stuff. I'm embarrassed enough as it is."

"Embarrassed?"

"I mean it, Will. We talk about the plane or Lancaster or I walk."

"Fine," he said through clenched teeth. "Ms. Binali, will you lend your skills to the United States government for the purpose of preventing a national security disaster?"

When he said it that way it made her want to

help, despite the impossibility of it all. "Do you have any way to narrow the search field?"

Will took a sudden interest in his boots before he finally looked her in the eye. "Not according to my last communication."

She started to explain the futility of it when he cut her off. "But you know where it is. When did Lancaster protest about the route you were taking?"

"Almost as soon as we left the parking lot."

Will shook his head. "I'm betting there were specific moments."

"Sure. He wanted to go due north when we were near the first challenge course."

"Because he was tracking the beacon. We can head north on a line from those spots and find the plane first."

"I've heard amazing stories from navy SEALs, but I didn't know they could walk on air." She ignored the frustrated furrow between his eyebrows, ignored her silly, girl-crush urge to soothe him. "The reason I led them around is because at that point the land runs out in a hurry. Going due north would've been a dangerous scenic route that dead-ends in a steep canyon."

"Damn." Will paced the short expanse of their camp with long legs and a quick stride. He rubbed one thumb across the opposite palm as he digested her news. "Do you recall anything they said about the beacon last night?"

"Only that it was still sending a strong signal." She shook her head. "I was preoccupied."

"I know." His eyes were full of such a deep understanding she wanted to cry. "I know you don't want to go back to see any of them, but if you aren't confident about cutting them off, that's our only option."

She marveled at the emotions battling inside her. Never big on drama, it surprised her to swing from angry and empowered to sorrow and utter defeat in the span of a few seconds.

Giving up, she sat down at the edge of the slope and let her gaze roam.

Clearly, the job mattered to Will. He'd given her enough details that she understood the importance of his mission. Though she was angry with him, she recognized his determination to succeed against the steep odds.

"Charly?"

She felt him hovering behind her, smart enough not to touch. "I'm thinking."

He sat down close by, and she did her best to ignore the sound of his breathing.

"Splitting up—" she began.

"Not an option," he said.

"Makes sense," she countered. "More eyes

covering more ground in the search for Lancaster's prize is sensib—"

"But—"

"Will, if you interrupt me again, our partnership is over and nothing you say or do will keep me from walking down this mountain." She waited, listening to her heartbeat and only her heartbeat for several long seconds. "I understand your concerns and the basic plan. Assuming you have the climbing skills, if we had the gear we could go due north and maybe with a lot of luck, find the plane."

She paused, gathering her thoughts, hating the words that had to be spoken. "If I'd taken a radio instead of a gun, things might be different. As it stands, you're right. We need to track Lancaster." It would be the greatest test of her self-control to watch and wait when she had Clint's murderer in her sights. "At least until we can narrow the search field."

Will remained silent.

"I'm done talking now," she declared.

"All right." His clothing rustled softly as he scooted up to sit beside her. "Before we even get started, I want to say thank-you." He bounced a fist on his thigh, then sighed. "It was my third op when it happened to me."

Sensing where this was going, Charly stiffened. She did not want to hear this. She didn't want to feel a connection. She needed her embarrassment over the lies he'd fed her in town, needed the anger to keep her steady.

"Just getting to graduation makes you feel immortal," he began, his voice barely a whisper. "We know in here—" he tapped his temple "—that certain actions are high risk. We know there are consequences when we go out."

She understood what he meant, though the context differed between civilian life and military action. There were risks when she helped on search and rescue, more risks when she helped track fugitives.

"Intel on the op was clear, complete as it gets. The plan was simple—get in, get our hostage, get out. But the bizarre happened in the form of an IED. We weren't even the target. Not really. We had the best training in the world, but I wasn't fully prepared for the weight of hauling my dying friend to the egress point."

Her mind drifted back to Clint's temporary grave.

"It's the strangest thing to see a man you've lived with, worked with, a man you consider a brother go down," Will continued. "It's worse when it feels senseless. I know how that sticks with you, Charly. But eventually you get through the grief and reach a point where you can recall the fullness of the life instead of the empty moment of death."

Steady? Her entire system was quaking like a leaf in a windstorm. She looked down at their joined hands. When had that happened? How was she supposed to maintain her composure after hearing a story like that? Feeling petty, she tugged her hand free. She wanted to call him a liar, to accuse him of manipulating her, but she couldn't get the mean words past the lump of tears lodged in her throat. Blinking rapidly, she pushed to her feet and buried the volatile mix of feelings whirling inside her.

It would take huge doses of calm and focus to get them through this. By sheer will, her vision was clear when she looked at Will again. "Let's go."

He stood up and dusted off his dark pants. "You've got the lead."

She nodded, choosing the most direct path. When Lancaster was in custody, when Will's job was complete and they were back in Durango, she'd take an entire day, maybe two, and wallow in her grief over Clint.

For now, they had work to do.

Chapter Ten

Will knew he'd handled things poorly with Charly, and with every silent step carrying them closer to Lancaster, he vowed to make it up to her when this was over. That kind of decision came with a new risk factor he'd never considered before, but the woman pulled things out of him. Things he never discussed. Yet he'd sat there and held her hand and let it pour out. Telling himself it was for her benefit, to ease her grief, was complete bull.

This kind of sticky situation proved why he was better working the solo operations. Working alone, he couldn't embarrass himself by sharing pitiful memories of his failures. Alone, he couldn't cause others the embarrassment he'd caused Charly.

Her reaction to his purpose up here surprised him. He'd expected the anger, but he couldn't see any reason for her to feel foolish over their dates. He just didn't know how to explain it to her in a way she'd understand.

Thank God they were finally close enough to Lancaster's camp that talking wasn't safe. Too often since they'd set off he'd wanted to apologize, to make his feelings for her clear. She hadn't misunderstood his interest, but he figured he'd have a hell of a time convincing her of that anytime soon.

This wasn't the best time to get distracted by the woman, so he gained a little detachment by focusing on her skills as a guide. Yesterday he'd discovered a serious appreciation for her endurance. Today, in closer proximity, he marveled at her commanding awareness of their surroundings—of all things nature.

As they'd become acquainted, she'd talked a little about her family and the traditions she carried forward with their business, but seeing her in action was nothing short of astounding. She moved swiftly, only occasionally glancing to the sky or pausing to listen to her surroundings. Granted, he knew she was familiar with the area, but watching her, he understood her grandfather's comment about her having a compass for a heart. Charly traveled with such confidence, without leaving a trace, that Will thought the military should hire her for training.

Without a word, she'd pointed out animal

tracks as they appeared. Both prey and predator, from rabbits and deer to wolves. Thank God the bears and snakes were hibernating. He wasn't so ignorant about the area that he thought Lancaster's crew was the only threat on this mountain, but he was suddenly grateful he was navigating this wicked terrain with Charly.

He didn't give an opinion on their route, trusting her to find the most direct path to the campsite. He wondered what they'd find when they got there. He hoped the men had left behind a few provisions. His small pack wasn't going to carry them very far.

Much as he'd done last night, she crossed the stream and circled around, avoiding the trail she'd cleared with Lancaster. To his surprise, Will heard men shouting as they closed in on the campsite. He couldn't believe Lancaster hadn't set out already.

With no more than a look, he and Charly dropped flat, carefully creeping forward to watch and listen.

"We have a signal from that beacon to follow," Lancaster shouted. "Forget the bitch. We don't need her."

One of the men was down and one eye was swollen shut.

Charly tapped him. "Jeff," she mouthed, pointing to the ground.

Will nodded, understanding. The man who'd been charged with guarding her last night hadn't fared well in the hours since her escape.

"If she notifies the authorities," another man said, "we're all screwed."

"I say we leave Jeff to deal with any authorities while we go on to the plane."

Will noted Jeff kept his opinion on that plan to himself.

"Dumb move going without her. She can't be far."

"We're not incompetent," said Max. He held up the tracking gear. "We know where we're going."

"But you saw how well she knows the area."

"Enough!" Lancaster stopped the bickering. "This isn't a damned democracy. You work for me," he said, his face turning red. "All of you work for me."

Watching the body language, Will thought the men surrounding Lancaster disagreed. It seemed as though Scott was the man the others looked to time and again for guidance.

"You want to get paid, you follow *my* orders."

Will slid a look toward Charly while Lancaster ranted on. She met his gaze with a raised-eyebrow expression that told him they were on the same page. A madman running around on the mountain was going to be a particular kind of fun.

"We'll split up," Lancaster said, only slightly calmer. "Jeff and Bob will track down the guide and kill her. The rest of us will go to the plane."

"And how do we find you when we're done?" Bob asked.

"You have radios. I can't imagine she's gone far. She must be panicked, knowing we won't let her get away. Find her. Kill her. If you're closer to Durango when that's done, you'll wait for us in town."

Will took it as small comfort that the crew planned to return to Durango after retrieving the Blackout Key. He'd pass that intel to Casey. The director could have a reception waiting for Lancaster.

Will carefully watched the men tasked with killing Charly. It was clear they thought they'd be cut out of the profit. At worst, they'd be in place as the scapegoats if things went bad up here.

It wasn't any surprise, but the division of Lancaster's crew meant a new set of challenges. He and Charly couldn't follow both Lancaster and the other men. He had no intention of leaving Charly out here alone. Not just because he needed her expertise to get around faster. Not just because her need to avenge Clint rolled off her in perilous waves.

No, his need to keep her close went deeper than that. He told himself it was the mission, that he wouldn't leave a civilian out here, unarmed and underequipped, to bat cleanup for the United States. He wasn't believing it. Still, he couldn't risk letting his mind wander down that path littered with land mines. Better to keep it all business up here.

Charly was a civilian, and considering how angry she was at him, it was best not to bring his personal interest into the mix. Dating her was fun and exciting, but he'd known from the start it wouldn't turn into anything long-term. He wasn't built for the long haul. Didn't have the heart for it.

Beside him, Charly didn't even twitch as they watched Jeff and Bob gather gear, check weapons and head away from the campsite. Again he thought SEAL candidates could learn a few things from her. In a town like Durango it hadn't taken long to learn about Charly's stellar reputation for guiding and tracking, but she'd been so lively and animated when they played pool or talked over a meal. He'd had no idea she had this deep well of cool reserve.

It took a remarkable person to remain still and calm in the face of such a direct and deadly threat. It took something else—an undefinable quality—to do so this close to a friend's rough grave.

Will struggled against an inexplicable need to rush in and take down the five men distracted with their preparations to move out. For Charly. He could see the solution and call it a good day's work. They could take the beacon and find the damned key, and be done with it all.

Only Casey's desire to take Lancaster alive, along with Will's combat experience, kept him in place next to her.

She shifted closer, and her fingertips landed with a light flutter on his hand. He hadn't realized he'd reached down for the gun holstered to his thigh. He gave her a brief nod, and she seemed to understand he had himself under control again.

It felt like an eternity before he risked a cautious whisper. "We're not splitting up," he said, offering her a hand up.

She didn't accept his offer of help, but she deliberately turned her back to Clint's grave. "We can tail Lancaster," she said, surprising him. "He's your priority."

"You aren't worried about the other two men?"

She shook her head. "Are you? Unless they're blind, they'll pick up the trail I left for them."

Her easy dismissal of the pair caught his attention. "What did you do?"

"I led them toward a natural trap. If we're really lucky one of the men who feels like this mountain is his personal property will intercept them first."

"And if we're not really lucky?"

"They'll turn north and try to rejoin Lancaster, pinning us in the middle."

"Why didn't you go to a mountain man for help last night?"

"I didn't need help last night until you tackled me."

He figured it best if he didn't reply directly to that.

She cocked an eyebrow, clearly understanding his silence. "Besides, I'd talked myself into going to the authorities, thinking that was better than conducting my own manhunt."

"Come on," he said, crossing the creek to the campsite. "Maybe they left us something useful."

She surprised him again when she didn't even pause at her friend's grave. But he turned when she swore softly. "If it wasn't your job to secure Lancaster, I'd say let the mountain take care of these guys."

He walked over and knelt down as she gathered up an open pack of fresh food. "Did you expect them to be responsible campers?"

"A girl can dream," she muttered while she dealt with it. "But I'm not surprised."

Charly bit back the rant. It wouldn't help and it was only a diversion from the real problem. She might be out of her depth with national security and the mailman-turned-SEAL, but she recognized that truth. It felt as if her veins were trembling with grief, anger and fear. None of that would bring Clint back. None of those feelings would see justice done for him. Especially not the fear.

She found her pack and examined what Jeff and his pals hadn't taken. Her spare radio was missing, but they'd left her first-aid supplies and the meal bars.

She left the tent behind. It was too cumbersome for what Will had in mind. "Check Clint's pack for any rope or gear," she said to Will. Once they had a better idea of where the plane went down, she wanted every advantage to get Will to the objective first.

Hearing Lancaster order her death, hearing the others agree so easily to carry out the order, something had clicked into place. If Lancaster thought he'd hired the best, he was about to find out how right he'd been. She shrugged into the small backpack and cinched the straps so it wouldn't shift. Lancaster thought he could run roughshod over this forest, over land she considered as vital as her heart. She'd happily show him how wrong he was.

She spared a final glance for Clint's grave, making a silent promise to return and bury him honorably at her first opportunity. She promised herself that despite the sharp and lethal odds stacked against her, she'd survive both Lancaster and the perils north of the peak.

"Ready?"

She nodded, not quite prepared to test her voice or meet Will's gaze. Ready to do this was the only option, because she refused to give in.

"Lead the way."

It wasn't much of a test. Lancaster, feeling safe, didn't care about hiding his trail. For the first hours, the real trick was holding back far enough that they didn't get caught.

There had been a call on the radio and another heated discussion about the route, forcing Charly and Will to fall back and discuss their options.

"Any ideas?"

"Might be entertaining when they try to walk on air."

"Entertaining," Will echoed, his eyebrows drawing close. "They must have some idea about the terrain."

"If so, they hid it well yesterday."

"They can check the area with their smartphones."

She shook her head. "Those are only expensive paperweights at this point."

"I'd think the beacon tracker would have some setting about terrain."

"Maybe." Charly swallowed the lump in her throat. "Clint got a look, said it was high-end. We didn't talk about it after that." Their time had run out. She felt Will's eyes on her, had just opened her mouth to fend off any sympathy when she caught the faint sound of voices.

Pressing her index finger to her lips, she drew them behind a screen of small trees. Rooted in place, absolutely still, she couldn't even hear Will's breathing.

Nearby, a radio crackled, but the disembodied voice on the other end was garbled. Beside her, she knew Will was straining for any clue about who was out there.

Bob's voice, slightly breathless, reached them just before he came into view.

Damn. She'd managed to get them pinned between Lancaster and the team he'd sent out to kill her. Why hadn't her trap worked? The strong and sudden urge to run surprised her. She had to smother it. Running wasn't an option. The men were too close.

Will touched her shoulder and the gentle contact grounded her. She scanned the area, looking for the best option for a fight or escape.

If they had any sense, the men should pass right by their hiding place.

"We should've gone back down," Bob said, stopping to catch his breath.

"I'm telling you she's out here somewhere," Jeff argued.

"You saw her hat. She's dead or long gone."

"I'm not staking my cut on your theory. That was a fake trail."

"No way. She was scared, is all. It was dark. She got lost." Bob swore. "And Scott knows better than to cut us out of the take. Besides, that mad bastard left too much behind in Durango. Let them freeze their asses off out here. It's easy enough to catch up with them when they're done."

She could see Jeff wasn't buying it. His eyes, one dark and bruised, scanned the forest floor, moving into the trees. Any second now and he'd spot them.

How had she missed his skills?

Because she hadn't been looking. Too busy operating on the assumption that she was leading curious software developers, she'd been focused on giving a good tour.

"She didn't get hurt, lost or dead," Jeff insisted. "It was a trap for whoever followed her."

A trap that failed, she thought with more than a little regret. Hopefully there'd be time to feel like an idiot about that later. Right now they had to start evening the odds.

She looked to Will, grateful one of them was dressed for stealth. She pointed to herself, indicated her plan to stand up and draw their attention. He could circle around and they'd have them.

Will gave a nearly imperceptible shake of his head.

She sent him a defiant glare, motioning for him to circle around.

He reached for his gun and this time she shook her head. They needed to handle this quickly and silently, without allowing Jeff or Bob to notify Lancaster.

She thought that kind of tactic would be second nature to a man with Will's professional experience. Grabbing his jacket, she pressed her mouth close to his ear and outlined her plan.

He was already nodding as she eased back. Good. He needed to trust her ability to handle herself and drop this archaic need to protect her at every turn. She would not allow herself to be a liability for him. Shifting, she made just enough noise to draw Jeff's attention.

"What was that?"

"Nature," Bob replied, bored. "I want hot food and a soft bed."

"It could be her." Jeff peered into the trees.

She waited, holding her breath until Will made his move.

"You're obsessed," Bob accused. He reached for his radio. "Let's find out where the hell the mad bastard is and catch up with them."

With a sturdy stick in her hand, she launched from her hiding place. A moment early, yes, but she couldn't let Lancaster learn that she was out here alive. With an ally like Will.

Will moved in a black blur, tackling Bob at the waist and plowing the man into the dirt.

Jeff turned, facing her when she'd been counting on taking him from behind. Didn't matter. Temper and fury simmered just under the surface of her skin, pushing her, making her strong. She saw the reaction in his eyes, the memory of what she'd done to him last night.

His hand slapped for his weapon holstered on his thigh and the hesitation made up for the ruined surprise attack.

Her heart sang with a warrior's pride as she slammed the stick she held against his jaw. The blow turned him, and she brought the stick hard across his throat and pulled back with both hands.

He clawed at her fingers, desperate to loosen her grip. She used her knee in his back as more leverage, willing him to go down before she crushed his windpipe.

Once more, thanks to her, he passed out. But this time when he came to, she wasn't giving him any good options.

"You okay?" Will asked, stalking over, his features clouded with temper.

"He didn't lay a finger on me."

"Good."

She looked past him to the prone form of the other man. "Did you kill him?"

"No." The single word carried a hefty dose of regret.

"But we should," he said. "It's the only way to be sure they won't escape and attack us again."

"I have a better idea. Take the radios and weapons. Search the packs. I'm sure there's something we can use to restrain them."

What their search of the packs revealed set her back, turning her blood to a cold sludge as she understood the implications. The pieces of menacing long-range rifles. The ammunition clips for the rifles and handguns. Explosives and detonators. They might have killed Clint early, but this trip would've definitely been her last.

"Mercenaries," Will said quietly. "They tend to have rough edges."

It made sense, but it didn't diminish the chill creeping along her skin.

"Want me to finish them?"

She shook her head, unwilling to leave that burden solely to him. "I'd rather they paid a harder price."

Chapter Eleven

It wasn't easy hauling the two men upstream and more than once Will was sure he'd made the wrong choice letting Charly talk him into this, but when Jeff and Bob were secure, he had to admit the plan had merit.

"Last chance," Charly said. "Tell us where the plane is."

Both men stared past her with hard eyes, their features set in stone. Will didn't expect either of them to crack, but he hadn't expected Charly to come up with this crazy idea, either.

"All right." She dialed a radio to an emergency setting and used the carrying strap to loop it over a branch well out of reach of the men. "We're leaving now," she said, standing back from where they'd trapped the men near the base of a small waterfall.

Jeff bellowed for help.

"Shout all you want," she told them as they

glared at her. "But I recommend you take the time to get your story straight before help arrives."

"Where did you come from?" Jeff glared at Will. "You're in over your head."

"Not the first time," Will said, walking away.

"We'll be on your tail by nightfall," Bob promised.

Will gawked at Charly's deadly smile as she leaned down close to Bob. "Best of luck with that."

Bob spat at her while Jeff swore. Will stepped up to defend her, but she didn't need his assistance.

She easily dodged Bob's assault and laughed at Jeff's threats. "Good luck, boys. And if you do break free, I recommend you follow the stream downhill and get yourself to safety. If you attack us again I'll help him—" she pointed over her shoulder at Will "—kill you both."

Sure-footed, she stalked back up the bank. Will tried to keep his mind away from her speech, but he couldn't quite keep his eyes off her shapely butt as it swayed from side to side in front of him.

When they were out of earshot, he laid a hand on her shoulder. "You meant it."

"About killing them if they attack again?"

He nodded.

"Better believe it."

"Then why not kill them now?" He knew he sounded bloodthirsty, but he was trying to figure out her thought process. He supposed he had the no-loose-ends philosophy in common with Lancaster. Not a comfortable thought, but reality was rarely comfortable.

"If they come after us again, it's on them," she replied. "Not orders, not financial reward, just them. Jeff showed a small measure of compassion last night. I returned the favor today."

"So the ball's in their court."

"That's how I see it."

Per his military training and absolute necessity, dead or alive, prisoners were contained. "You're sure they can't escape?" He didn't want to get pinched between Lancaster and these two again, regardless of her newfound willingness to end their lives.

"They can try."

The men were at a significant disadvantage. Will had their weapons and flashlight, and the one radio was well out of reach. They'd wasted enough time giving the pair a chance to live. He needed to drop the subject and resume his mission: getting to the plane.

"The park rangers should come through within a day."

"What? A day?" He'd thought a few hours at best. This was getting better all the time. "You're telling me they'll be out here all night?"

"Yes. And I wish we could watch them squirm in the cold and wet, but we need to catch up with Lancaster."

"Remind me never to cross you."

He caught her sideways look, the arched eyebrow and the little smirk on her lips.

"It wouldn't be in your best interest," she admitted, picking up the pace.

He wanted to revel in the moment, but another problem weighed on his mind. "What if those two convince the park rangers you're responsible for their condition?"

"I hope they try. That would only make the rangers more curious." Her shoulders jerked up and down. "A bizarre claim versus my reputation? Not a chance. The rangers know me. With you backing my story, the weapons we found and Clint?" Her voice cracked on her friend's name and she went quiet for a few minutes. "Those two can't say anything that will hurt me or the business. Even if they tried, one of my brothers is a lawyer."

"Good to know. I guess we'd better stick together then."

She stopped short. "You were right about that. I get it now."

"That's not why I said it," he said, striding up to join her.

"Relax, Will. I just thought you should know you won't get any further argument from me on that."

"Oh." He knew he should be happy about her cooperation. He should've noticed her attitude shifting to line up with Casey's agenda. Instead, he'd been distracted by the woman under the impressive, cool facade. So far the only thing to crack was her voice when she thought of her friend and trail partner.

They trekked on at a brisk pace and moved faster without the burden of two prisoners. He had the radio, but it remained silent. They weren't retracing their steps back to Lancaster's campsite; she was guiding them around it. Smart, he thought. A direct route was easy, but easy often led to more trouble. In this situation, he had to believe Lancaster and his men would stick with areas they knew.

"You would've been an asset to the navy SEAL program."

Her laughter bubbled around him. "That's ridiculous."

"Not so much," he replied. "You're unflappable."

"Out here, maybe." She stopped, frozen in place, and held out a hand so he would do the same.

He listened, unable to pin down anything other than the sounds of nature all around them. Though he wanted to ask, he kept his mouth shut, following her gaze in search of what had startled her. Sunlight lanced through the trees, the light and shadows dancing with the gentle breeze.

From his perspective, they had the advantage. Trees down the slope, a clear view across an open snowfield at their backs. He couldn't see anything, couldn't hear any trouble. But something had her spooked.

Suddenly bullets marched across the trees he thought were fair cover, tearing at bark and branches in vicious bites.

They both dropped to hands and knees behind the wide fanning branches of a spruce tree. He pushed her back and up, away from the shooter. The radio crackled and the man named Scott gave instructions to someone else. "Two targets. Two. Someone is with her."

"Two targets," one of the others confirmed.

Will exchanged another look with Charly. They didn't know if they were up against the whole party or a scouting team. No time to assess as more bullets came at them. Not a lucky volley in a random attack, he realized. He got up, setting off at a dead run and drawing the fire away from her.

It worked, but there wasn't much time to celebrate the success. He was running out of trees, being chased into the open of the high snow plain. If he gave in, made a dash for it, he had to assume there was a sniper in place to take him out. He hated admitting it, but somehow the enemy had gained an advantage.

Dirt and bark flew, following Charly as she came at him.

"What are you doing?"

"We stay together."

He shook his head. "Not this time."

"I saw Scott. Do you think they're all together?"

"Does it matter?" They had her revolver, his handgun and the weapons taken from Jeff and Bob. Will worried it wouldn't be enough.

"Guess not." She crouched, ducking for cover at another three-round burst. She inched close enough to whisper in his ear, "We have to cross that plain. Head over the ridge."

He frowned down at her and shook his head. It was a killing field for sure. There was too much space between them and the closest shelter. "We'll be sniper fodder," he said. It was too easy to picture the white snow splashed with blood. Her blood.

"We can't go forward."

"I can flank him."

"No."

She was going to run for it. He saw it in her eyes an instant before she made the first move. A certain death trap, he thought as he laid down cover fire in a last-ditch effort to protect her.

But the cover fire he directed at Scott did nothing to stop the sniper from taking aim at Charly. Worse, as he raced after her he realized their tracks through the snow left a clear trail for anyone to follow. Assuming either of them survived long enough to be hunted.

"Find cover!" he shouted at Charly. He skidded behind the shelter of a boulder, his eyes tracking the tree line, then higher, looking for the logical sniper's roost.

Too many options, he realized, as he tucked away his pistol and readied the rifle he'd taken off Bob. Will saw Scott strolling along the leading edge of the trees, but he wasn't about to waste another bullet. When he pulled the trigger next time, he wanted it to count for more than a diversion.

Waiting for his opening or the sniper's next bullet, he let his mind drift across his past. He'd been in worse situations. Probably. There had certainly been other instances when national security had been on the line. Other times when he'd worked solo to protect civilian interests.

"Take your time," he murmured, his cheek pressed to the stock. He drew in a long, slow breath, calming his heart rate. "I've got all day."

He couldn't fail. Not just because Casey was counting on him to stop Lancaster's deadly, self-centered quest for vengeance. Not just because he wanted to live past this particular mission. More than either of those salient points, he flat-out refused to fail Charly. She needed an ally to get off this mountain alive.

He should've let her go for help. He could've drawn them away from her. But his mission focus, colored by urgency and no small amount of pride, had kept them out here.

It was too late to send her back alone. Her skills were superb, but Lancaster's men were proving themselves more adept out here than Will had anticipated. The marksmanship didn't surprise him. Nor did the cold-blooded nature of the mercenaries Lancaster had hired. The tenacity…that was a bigger problem.

Lancaster didn't want loose ends. That much was clear. But Lancaster's team hadn't met Will's determination. He would do this job. He'd own it. Not just for Casey or the nation at large, but for Charly.

The awareness trickled into him like cool water sliding down his throat after a grueling week in the desert. He hadn't felt this type of personal connection with anyone since his brother died. He hadn't needed anything else. Hadn't been sure he was useful to anyone beyond the job anymore.

Charly was making him reevaluate.

As seconds ticked by, turning into several minutes without any gunfire, Will compared the few options available to both sides.

Based on previous behavior, Scott and whoever was sniping for him wouldn't stray far from Lancaster. The Blackout Key was too valuable and from what he'd overheard so far, Lancaster needed the mercenaries to get away cleanly.

Through the rifle's scope, Will had a close-up view of Scott as he answered the radio. He couldn't hear the conversation, but the scowl gave him an idea of how well the exchange was going.

Scott grew more agitated and started to pace. Will squeezed off two shots, but didn't get to enjoy the reaction as the sniper got a bead on his position. Bullets ricocheted but didn't find their mark, and he heard Scott call out a retreat. Will watched for movement and cursed the well-trained team when he still couldn't spot the sniper.

Through the scope he saw Scott wrapping some kind of tape around his lower leg. A minor injury would have to be enough for today. Will turned away from the trees, eager to check on Charly. Noting the blood spattered across the snow, his heart lodged in his throat. Somehow he managed to call her name as he staggered to his feet.

Snow exploded to his right, and Charly's voice erupted from his left. "Get down!"

She leaped at him, grabbing his coat and hauling him down as they went sliding across a snow-covered slope. They gained speed on the incline like a runaway sled. Adjusting, Will turned so they were going feetfirst instead of sideways. One arm holding Charly, he tried to grasp for anything to slow them down with the other. He lost the rifle in the process, but was more concerned about losing her.

There was no cover, and he was sure the sniper would pick them off any second. Another rock speared up from the snow, and Will said a prayer it would stop them as he braced for the impact.

It held. Thank God.

"Are you hurt?"

"No," she said, breathless. "You?"

"There was blood back there. On the snow," he added, looking her over from head to toe. He couldn't see any wounds, though her clothing had taken a beating. "It isn't yours?"

"Unlucky rabbit, probably."

Her answer left him speechless and beyond grateful she was okay.

"Come on, we have to keep moving." She rolled to her feet, tugged on him to urge him along.

"Where are we?" The snow here was more like a thin, icy layer dusting rocks and stubborn plants.

"We slid into a dried-up creek bed. This way."

"They'll be on our trail fast."

"I know," she said, legs churning as she ran. "Hurry."

He grabbed his pistol as they moved, trying to keep up with her as she crossed the rocky ground with the confidence of a mountain goat. He heard the shouts of pursuit and glanced back, relieved the rocks disguised their trail. If they could just get out of sight, they had a chance.

He'd no more thought it than Charly disappeared behind an outcropping. Following, he squeezed between two boulders and into a shallow recess in the mountainside. Not enough space to qualify as a cave, there was barely room for their packs and bodies. She was pressed against him from shoulder to thigh, and he hoped like hell it was enough shelter to keep them hidden. Between the adrenaline and Charly, his system was completely revved. He tried to dial it down, but knew it wasn't working. "Best bet is to wait them out."

"We'll stay here until nightfall," she murmured. "Then we can move."

"Agreed." He could only be grateful the daylight hours were short this time of year.

She trembled, and it might have been his body shivering, they were so close. "Are you cold?"

"I'll be fine."

Her husky reply tested the thinning tether he had on the desire pumping through him. He only had to make it to nightfall.

Peering up at the sky, he told himself it was possible. Possible to ignore her soft curves pressed against him. Possible to forget the sweet taste of her lips. He had to find another line of thought.

He wanted to get up, to shake his head and clear out the sensual haze, but he couldn't risk moving and giving the shooter another target.

"Will?"

"Hmm?"

"Thanks for the cover fire."

"Anytime," he replied.

A quiet giggle shook through her and into him. "It's fine with me if it's just this once."

"You've got a deal."

"From this side of the ridge, we should be able to get a lead on Lancaster's route."

"How do you figure?"

"He can't get due north without climbing gear. I didn't see any in Jeff or Bob's packs."

"Could be one person is carrying the load for all of them."

"Maybe so," she allowed.

"How will *we* get to the plane without climbing gear?"

"That depends."

He hesitated to ask. "On what?"

"What's in your pockets."

"Pardon?"

"If you have binoculars, I know of an overlook in that general direction that might allow us to get in front of Lancaster."

"How can you see anything up here?" So much of it looked the same to him. Vast and beautiful. Steep slopes of green and brown broken by sparkling water, outcrops of stone, even caps of snow up here in these higher elevations. Without a beacon or an overhead view, he couldn't fathom how she'd find a small downed aircraft. "This is the ski resort side of the range, right?"

"Yes. Why?"

"I was thinking about the plane's possible

destination. Maybe somewhere nearby was a fueling stop or something."

"That could be any number of places along here, or well west. Are you thinking of contacting the local airfields?"

"Maybe. What if Lancaster tried to rent a helicopter before he came to you?"

"I can't image any pilot agreeing to search without a specific destination."

"True. But with the beacon, he could've given a decent search field."

"So if he gave a pilot general coordinates and still had to come to me…" Her voice trailed off, and her eyes scanned the little slice of sky they could see from their hiding place.

"You do know where he's headed. I knew you'd figure it out."

"I don't know precisely," she admitted, "but that does give me a better idea. There's a lot of treacherous ground to cover and at least five men determined to get there before you."

"One of them isn't walking well."

"Go team us," she mused.

But she didn't sound too enthused. He rubbed her knee. The risk to his sanity was worth it. "We'll get there first," he said, dragging his mind back to the problem instead of the woman.

"Don't get too confident," she warned.

"Why wouldn't I be confident? You're like an ace up my sleeve." Something about her gave him more than confidence. She gave him real hope.

Chapter Twelve

Charly felt as though they'd been cramped for years in the tiny crevice rather than the hours it had taken for the sun to set. They'd listened to the chatter on the radio between Scott and Lancaster, debating who'd been with Charly and how to contain them. Lancaster had been furious at Scott's failure, but called them back to move on with their primary purpose.

Will had called her his secret ace, but she was thinking the reverse was true. He'd been right that this crew was more dangerous, more desperate than she'd first thought.

Charly didn't like moving at night, not on this side of the ridge, where any step could knock debris loose and give away their position. Or worse, send them tumbling down to rocks below. But they couldn't stay out here, exposed, with only her sleeping bag and each other as shelter against the elements.

Her brain stalled out, savoring the images

that flooded her mind with that thought. Totally inappropriate thoughts, considering their life-and-death predicament. It smelled like snow and while she didn't expect a big accumulation this time of year, even a dusting could be enough to slow them down.

They had to get ahead of Lancaster and his crew. They'd just escaped a barrage of bullets and yet part of her was consumed by the urge to get her hands on Will's rock-hard pecs and ripped abs. It was embarrassing. They needed to find a safe place to wait out the snowfall and regroup. Her distraction would mean an advantage for Lancaster if she didn't pull herself together.

"What do you think?"

She looked up at Will, standing by her side as she faced the vast emptiness just beyond their feet, where the mountain gave way to a steep, rugged canyon. His chiseled features were blurred by darkness, his eyes impossible to read.

"I think we need to take the chance." She reminded herself that he'd trusted her to deal with Jeff and Bob. It was time to trust him and his training.

Will took another step, peering over the edge. "Some chance."

She knew he was thinking about the stingy length of rope in her pack. Neither of them was geared up for real climbing. Under normal circumstances, she believed they were both smart enough to *not* do what she'd suggested. But they had to survive. The night, the weather, Lancaster.

"This cliff is riddled with caves. It's our best bet to get through the night."

He looked around, and she could practically feel the realization dawning. "Cliff. Caves. Under us, yes?"

"Yes." One wrong move and— She couldn't let her mind wander any closer to the negative. "I can get us there. We'll have shelter, a break from the wind and snow."

"They won't expect us to go over."

"And it should give us a safe vantage point when they set out in the morning," she added, keeping her voice low to match his. Having spent the day hiding, they didn't know how much progress Lancaster had made toward the beacon. In the dark, with no sign of a campfire, she and Will decided to go forward rather than search out their campsite.

"It'll work."

She wished she knew for sure, but as fat snowflakes began a slow descent, time for debate was over. If they waited any longer, she wouldn't be able to justify the risk. "This way." She checked the straps on her pack, tugged at Will's for good measure.

"It's not going anywhere," he assured her.

With a mental cross of fingers, she dropped to her butt at the cliff's edge and let her feet dangle in the wide abyss of dark. She supposed that was one small positive, not being able to see the distance from here to the bottom.

Will sat beside her and covered her hand with his. "Lead the way."

His absolute faith rattled her almost as much as it bolstered her confidence. This was the worst time to feel off balance, when she'd be scooting down a nearly invisible "stairway" with unyielding mountain on one side and nothing but air on the other.

"Okay. Down about six to eight feet," she began. "It's barely a ledge and I can't see the gaps well in the dark," she warned.

"Slow going. Got it."

She didn't give herself a chance to think about the benefit of anchors and ropes. Those things would only be a road map for Lancaster's crew in the morning.

Will tapped her on the shoulder, but she'd heard the same sound he had. Too big to be anything but one of Lancaster's men. At this point she had no doubt whoever it was would shoot first and sleep well after.

As if answering her thoughts, a gunshot blasted out of the darkness.

Strange how her basic instinct to survive debated her lousy choices. Bullets or canyon floor? No time. She relegated the panic and defeatist thoughts to the back of her mind as she pushed herself over the edge and prayed her feet would find purchase on the narrow lip of rock that had been worn down by wind and rain.

Her mind whipped through the math as she slid, clinging to the mountain as it bit into her side. Only six to eight feet. *Only.* She should feel the ledge under her toes within a second or two.

She didn't.

Just their luck if she'd chosen to go over at a new gap in the ledge. But she knew this mountain. The ledge should be there. What was the worst that could happen? One of the scrappy trees would catch them.

Her fingers dug into loose rock and soil before her toes, straining for contact, found the narrow lip of solid rock. She nearly laughed aloud in pure relief. A moment later, Will landed beside her.

"Go, go, go," he urged, his hand on her pack, keeping her close to the cliff.

She glanced up and got a face full of dirt knocked loose by the men chasing them. Scrambling, belly pressed to the side of the cliff, she moved as fast as she dared. Faster, as shouts tumbled down from above.

The wind spun snow around her face, coming down heavy enough now to give her a pale outline of their immediate surroundings. She ducked under a scruffy tree, gave Will plenty of warning about the obstacle and kept going.

The wide beam of a flashlight speared through the dark, wrecking her night vision. She studied the terrain as the light swept back and forth, determined to make it to shelter before the men above them found their aim.

A strange crack and wail had her turning back, panicked that Will had slipped. The scruffy tree between them was bending under the weight of one of Lancaster's men. Rich, she remembered, as the flashlight illuminated his terrified face.

For a moment, she was frozen, a helpless bystander amid the swirling cries for help and the promises of death.

"Go!" Will shouted.

She couldn't. Wouldn't leave him to deal with this alone. Without her guidance Will couldn't get to safety, and waiting only gave Lancaster a better chance to shoot them. It was either help Rich or they all lose. The panicked man in the tree swore as the shallow roots jerked and gave.

"Give me your hand," she said to Rich with a calm she used for emergencies.

"Don't do it," Will shouted. "Let me. I'm stronger."

Someone on the cliff's edge held the flashlight steady, painting the horrible tabloid in a weak spotlight with snowflakes floating through like pale confetti.

"Kill them," Lancaster called, his voice colder than the bitter night air.

The man tested her humanity. She'd like to show Lancaster who had a clear shot in this instance—her—but Will was adamant about taking him in alive.

"Reach for me," Will ordered the man.

"Can't," Rich said, clinging to the tree.

"You can," she told him. If she could catch his jacket, she might be able to swing him to the ledge.

The tree lurched free of the mountain a bit more as Rich struggled. "Oh, God."

"Stretch!" Will barked.

To her horror, bullets chattered around them, followed by more dirt and debris from above. She heard shouts from the men fighting among themselves, but her eyes were locked on Will and Rich. She braced to help in any possible way.

Rich reached, his hand connecting with

Will's. For a single heartbeat, she knew life would triumph. Then it changed.

Bullets marched through Rich and the snow, illuminated by the flashlight, turned into a red haze of blood. Will couldn't hold him, and the man and the scruffy tree tumbled away into the darkness.

"Move!" Will filled her vision, urging her along. She caught the muzzle flash of his gun as he fired off a few rounds to cover their retreat.

The light doused, by choice or bullet, she was blind, feeling her way with toes and fingers and memory. With a prayer, she scurried faster than was smart down the ledge, her slips and slides the only way to tell Will what was coming. Better to let the mountain take her than Lancaster.

She ducked into the shelter of the first cave and they sank back, waiting for any pursuit.

"They've given up for tonight," he said after a few minutes. "Can you keep going?"

It felt as if every cell in her body shivered. Wouldn't ever stop shivering. "Yes," she replied, victorious that she'd kept the word steady.

"I want more distance, if there's another safe place nearby."

"This side is full of caves. We can find another. Just—" She paused, covered her eyes with her cold hands. "Just let my eyes recover a minute."

"Takes longer than a minute," he said.

"I know." She took a deep breath. "But humor me anyway."

"Sure."

Opening her eyes, she walked back to the cave entrance. With a big breath, she started out once more. Stupid or brave, didn't matter—they couldn't stay put—so she moved swiftly along to the next cave big enough for both of them. "Is this better?" she asked.

Will waited again, listening, before joining her and escaping the reach of the elements. Turning on his flashlight, he scanned the empty space. "Perfect." The light went out and his voice drifted over her. "You're amazing. Charly, that was… I just don't know what to say."

She grabbed the straps of his pack and pulled him close, until his lips landed on hers. The contact wasn't gentle. Nothing close to seductive. It was a raw celebration of survival. He wrapped his arms around her, pulling her against his solid body, chasing the chill from her blood.

She changed the angle, her lips parting, tongue seeking his taste and heat. Clutching his shoulders for balance, she let desire and lust burn away the grim reality of their narrow escape.

There was nothing for her outside of this moment. Nothing in her world but him. Them.

Strong, steady and capable, Will became her gravity. She knew she'd float away without him.

She pushed at the straps of his pack, wanting to get her hands on all of him. Right *now*. Who knew how much time they had left? She wouldn't let this opportunity pass. Her palm slid across his chest, felt the heavy thud of his heart, and her pulse pounded an echo in her ears.

"I need you," she murmured against his lips while her fingers worked at his jacket. "Now."

"HANG ON." WILL leaned back from her sweet, soft mouth. Everything inside him wanted to seize what her body offered. Sure, there was plenty of mutual attraction on both sides, but he didn't want to be one more regret for her to deal with when the adrenaline faded.

He cradled her head to his shoulder and murmured some nonsense he hoped was soothing. "Let's just breathe a minute. We need to slow this down." That sounded pretty good. Almost reasonable.

"Sure." But she kept her hands fisted in the fabric of his jacket.

"We should start a fire."

"I've got plenty of fire for both of us." She pressed her lips together as she backed up a step, released him. "No fire. It could easily give away our position."

And he would've thought of that if she hadn't just fried his brain with that kiss. It was all he could do to stay sane enough to think past the desire.

She shrugged out of her pack and took her sleeping bag deeper into the dark cave. He heard the rustling as she rolled it out. "Warmer back here," she said.

"Good." He was hoping the cold air at the mouth of the cave would be as effective as a cold shower. "I'll take first watch."

"Get back here and get some rest," she suggested. "I'll wake up before dawn to watch for their movement."

"Charly."

"Worried I'll jump you?"

"The reverse, actually."

"If only," she said. "Flattering as that is, we're going to need each other—body heat—to get through the night without a fire."

He knew she was right even as he racked his brain for a suitable argument. He needed distance. Physically and emotionally. "Let's pretend it's another date. You owe me one anyway."

"I owe you a game of pool."

"And some conversation to go with it," he said. His feet felt like concrete blocks as he walked back to her. The date idea was solid.

They'd talk and pretend to be anywhere but a dark, cold cave until she fell asleep.

He set aside his pack and sat down at the edge of her sleeping bag. Loosening the laces of his boots, he pulled them off and changed into dry socks before he leaned back against the wall of the cave.

"I'm not sure I'm good for conversation," she said. The zipper of the sleeping bag rasped as she spread it out. "Why don't you start? We've talked about my family, but not yours."

Good grief. How did he get through this minefield? His date idea had twisted back and bitten him on the ass. As much as he didn't want to discuss his broken family, it would at least serve as an effective mood killer. Being honest about his past would kill any chance he had with her if—*when*—they got out of this increasingly frustrating Lancaster situation.

"We need to figure out how to find the plane," he mumbled.

"Can't do anything until the morning," she replied. "You know I have two brothers," she said. "Do you have siblings?"

"That's first-date chatter."

"It's the best I've got right now."

Will reminded himself patience was his strong suit. Patience had carried him through hell week. Vast wells of patience had seen him through ops that went perfectly and those that had gone sideways.

Here, with Charly in the line of fire, his patience was tapped. He wanted nothing more than to put this deadly game of cat and mouse behind him. He wondered if he could find a way back up there and just take Lancaster and his crew out tonight.

And they both knew he'd dodged the more personal questions whenever they were together. He saw her moving—felt it, really, a more substantial form among the heavy shadows. He could chat. Keep it light and easy. An easy task when he wouldn't have to face her reactions.

His pulse kicked as she settled next to him, her hip pressed against his. She drew the sleeping bag up across their legs, casting her scent over him. Sunshine and moss. The strange combination was soothing. Between her body and the sleeping bag, he wanted to sink into the comfort.

He had enough decency, self-control and, yes, patience, to deal with it.

"I had a brother." And parents, too, until Jacob died. "Do you ever wish your brothers put as much into the business as you do?"

"Sure. But we're talking about you right now."

"We are?"

She linked her hand with his. "Yes."

He heard the edge in her voice and knew he was stuck. She wanted him to open up. It wasn't as if she didn't deserve a little honesty. He could do this. "My brother died."

"I'm sorry." For a long time, the only sound was her soft breath. "I didn't realize how little I knew about you," she added. "Personally."

Well, crap. He couldn't help but wish for a rewind button. Only an idiot stopped a beautiful woman. Right about now they could be riding the crest of that adrenaline rush, the world's problems forgotten. If he hadn't put a halt to that kiss, she'd be naked under him now, incapable of forming words, much less giving voice to uncomfortable questions.

"Not much to know," he said, determined to keep it light. "All-American kid heads into the navy, gets cocky and somehow makes it through to become a SEAL."

"You never struck me as cocky."

"Huh." She had no idea how much he'd changed in recent years. "I'd better work on that."

"All right." Her soft laugh echoed through the cave. "New question. When was your first kiss?"

"Kindergarten," he confessed. "By the swings at the end of recess. She had blond pigtails and a frog on her shirt."

"Wow. Impressive memory."

"Some things you don't forget." And other things you couldn't forget no matter how much you wanted to. Jacob's face drifted through his mind.

"I bet you dated cheerleaders and homecoming queens."

Wary now, he hesitated. "Don't tell me guys weren't falling all over you growing up."

"Only in rugby."

"You played rugby?"

"Two seasons," she said with pride. "Keeping up with my brothers."

He'd pay good money to see those videos. "Bet you were good at it."

"I brought home my share of scrapes and bruises."

She didn't ask, but he heard himself answering. "My brother and I came up in soccer and eventually made the shift to baseball." He rubbed the scar on his chin. "Funny story. I got clipped by a bat in practice. My mom was scared of football…" His voice trailed off. She hadn't been big on sending her boys into the military, either, but he and his father had assured her all would be well. He remembered when she'd looked at him with pride shining in her eyes. But that sweet memory had been blotted out by the blame and sorrow overflowing her gaze from the other side of his brother's grave.

"My brother joined the marines," he heard himself whisper. Why didn't he just talk about something trivial, like taking the homecoming queen to the dance his senior year? "He told our parents he was inspired by me."

"Can you tell me what happened?"

He swallowed. "Worst-case scenario." It still sat like an elephant on his chest when he thought about it. Which was why he didn't think about it. "It was a training accident. He was the less than two percent of training casualties no one talks about. No one's fault, just…"

"The fluke that could've happened to anyone, but it happened to your family."

"Yeah." How was it she understood?

"I've seen my share of life, Will," she replied, making him wonder if he'd given voice to his question. "Up here you can do everything right and still get screwed over."

"My parents haven't spoken to me since the funeral."

She shifted, one hand stroking up and down his arm in a soothing touch. "You can't be serious."

He wished he wasn't. Wished he could shut up. "My kind of work doesn't make it easy to stay in touch anyway," he said.

"You're stateside now," she pointed out briskly.

"True."

"Ah. They don't know. You haven't told them."

He didn't like how easily she figured him out. Smart or not, it wasn't something he wanted to discuss. "This is all a little heavy for a cave-date conversation."

She gave his shoulder a light thump. "Maybe it's time to stop running away."

She was right, but he didn't have to like it. "It was easier to work. I couldn't fix it, couldn't change what happened. Still can't."

"How long has it been?" She raised their joined hands and pressed a soft kiss to his scraped knuckles.

Her compassion, along with her courage, was a force he couldn't stand against. "Long enough to be a habit."

"Will."

The gentle censure tugged at the protective walls he'd built around his heart. If she brought them down, he had no idea what would happen. To him or her if he couldn't defend her. This was the worst time and place for an emotional breakdown. He searched for a way to get back to something lighthearted. "Enough about me. When was your first kiss?"

"Sophomore year."

"High school?" He turned toward her, though

he couldn't get a read on her expression. "That's impossible."

"I'm sure it would've been sooner if I'd worn frog T-shirts."

He laughed and felt the heavy burden of grief easing inexplicably. "Hey, I'm a guy. We have standards."

"I noticed," she said, her voice full of appreciation. She cleared her throat. "First heartbreak?"

He wasn't sure anything could compete with the pain of losing his brother. They'd been so close, shared everything along the way. "Sally Bowman," he decided. Romantically, it was the closest he'd ever come to falling in love. "She ditched me at the homecoming dance to make out with the quarterback."

"Poor Will."

He didn't hear much sympathy in her tone. It made him smile. "And you?"

"I've had a few crushes along the way, but no one took enough interest to sweep me off my feet or break my heart."

The male population of Durango was stupid or blind. Maybe both. It sounded as though romantic neglect might qualify as a unique kind of heartbreak all on its own.

"Will?"

"Yeah?"

"If I told you I had a frog T-shirt with me, would you kiss me again?"

"Not tonight." It was too dangerous. Not mission danger—he was used to that. But he was far too vulnerable where she was concerned. Letting his desire get out of hand would erode his success on the mission.

"All right." She slipped away, burrowing under the sleeping bag and hunching her shoulders.

"Charly." He knew he should explain how much he wanted her. This just wasn't the right time to act on it. There had to be a way to assure her. He felt terrible that she would lump him into the category of the other guys who'd overlooked her.

"It was worth asking." She stretched her legs out and then curled up once more. "Come here so we both stay warm tonight."

He stretched out beside her, his body curving around hers. It was almost too much as she pillowed her head on his biceps. He told himself the layers of clothing were a good thing as he breathed deep of the enticing mountain scents caught in her hair.

"Get some sleep." She reached back and patted his thigh. "I'll wake us up in plenty of time to get ahead of Lancaster."

Chapter Thirteen

True to her word, Charly woke Will in plenty
of time. Based on the lack of noise nearby, Lancaster's crew wasn't moving yet. Standing at the
edge of the cave, Will gazed out across a bank
of fog that looked thick enough to walk across.
He pulled out the cell phone, waited for it to
power up, only to confirm there was no signal.
He turned it off and tucked it away, determined
to try again later.

To the east, the sun teased the horizon, but it
wouldn't be strong enough to burn through the
low-lying cloud for hours. His binoculars were
useless. The radio had been quiet all night. Will
checked the battery, skimming through other
channels, only to hear more silence.

"We should go," Charly said, hitching her
pack onto her shoulders. "If we stay quiet we
can get ahead of them."

"Go where? We can't see well enough to get
out of here."

"Which means they can't see well enough to shoot at us."

"That didn't stop them last night."

"True." She planted her hands on her hips. "The climb down is tedious work."

"In moist conditions with no gloves, chalk or safety gear."

She cocked her head, squinting at him as though he was a newfound species. "I thought military types like you would see the fun in that kind of challenge."

Only if his life was the only one on the line. "It wouldn't be my first time saving a civilian from stupidity," he teased.

Her eyebrows shot up in mock horror and he relaxed, grateful they'd found their way back to a friendly rapport after last night's sharefest. "And here I was hoping for a chance to add 'saved a SEAL' to my résumé." She put it in air quotes, making him smile. "Seriously, there's an easier way around from this point."

"Around what?"

"The cliff."

"Did you call in a helicopter?"

"No good in that." Waving at the fog, she walked away from the mouth of the cave. "Come on. Trust me."

He did. Completely. Not the way he trusted his fellow SEAL team members, but in a way that went deeper. Deeper into territory he'd never explored with a woman.

Following her and the pale white beam of her flashlight into a narrow tunnel of rock barely wide enough for his shoulders, he was reminded of his brother.

Growing up they'd gone off without thinking about anything beyond the thrill of the moment, hell-bent on whatever adventure they'd cooked up. He trusted Charly that same way—on instinct. She hadn't steered him wrong or given him any cause to think she would.

The rock fell away in places, as though someone had carved out windows. He sucked in a breath at the views. The valley below still blurred by the fog, another mountain peak speared up, looking close enough to touch. He couldn't feel the breeze, but he got a sense of it as fog poured in between the peaks, filling the valley like a giant sink.

"My guess is the plane crashed into the side of that ridge. Across the valley."

"Why?"

"Pilot error, quirky thermals, you name it." She rolled her shoulders, fiddled with the straps. "I can't be sure, but based on what you've said and Lancaster's behavior with the beacon, it fits."

He pulled out his binoculars, searching the opposite peak for any hint of a crash. He couldn't see anything definitive. "Take a look," he said.

She raised the military-grade black lenses to her eyes, making a small humming sound as she adjusted and swept as much of the terrain as the weather allowed. Then she stepped out, swiveled the glasses back toward the cliff they'd slid down last night. "Vultures," she said, pointing. "Probably circling the man who fell last night."

He noticed she didn't use the name. He wasn't inclined to provide it. Everyone dealt with trauma and loss in their own way. If avoiding the name made it easier for her to deal with the shock and the brutal after effect, that was fine by him.

"Unless something like a deer or horse is also dead over there."

"Maybe the vultures will discourage Lancaster." But he doubted anything would keep the man from his revenge. "How many times have you been up here for pilots?" He wanted her thinking of other things, things that she had more power over. Things that might have happy endings.

"A few."

"Any of them crash into this side?"

"Not traveling westbound."

"Okay." So she was giving him a well-educated guess. Not that he expected anything less.

"Best route for us?"

She pointed. "This area is more like a serrated knife with ups and downs of varying degrees between these peaks. At the base of this cliff we can head upstream and cross the water where it's shallow. Then it's just a matter of finding something useful."

"Or we're back to tailing Lancaster." Come on, universe. Would it be so terrible to catch a little luck on this op? They were surviving, but only by small margins. He wanted to make some progress today.

"I hope it doesn't come to that," she muttered.

He agreed. So much cleaner to grab the Blackout Key and disappear, letting nature have its way with Lancaster and his mercenaries. Too bad Casey wanted the jerk alive. "Lancaster will head straight for the crash site. Any idea how he'll get down here?"

She snorted. "His men will be lucky if he doesn't test their ability to fly across." She cleared her throat. "The best way down is south of where we scaled the cliff last night." She paused again. "After losing a man that way, I can't imagine anyone else on his crew will be willing to go over the cliff face like we did. That delay alone should give us at least another hour's lead time to find the plane."

"All right. How do we get down there?"

A corner of her mouth tipped up. Tempting him to taste, to take. He'd missed a golden opportunity by halting things last night. He reminded himself where that kiss would've led, and how unfair that result would be to her. She deserved better than a guy who could only give her a moment's pleasure. She deserved a man who wasn't afraid of giving her everything. A man who had everything to give.

"We follow the stairs."

"Stairs?" he echoed.

"They aren't up to code and yes, they're bound to be slippery with this fog, but they are functional."

"Duly noted."

He shouldn't have been shocked that her description was spot-on. The mountainside gave way incrementally from their cave to the valley below. There were slips and some mighty big steps, but overall, their trek down was uneventful.

The fog still hadn't shifted and the visibility was terrible. Though the sun had to be working on it by now, he wasn't sure which would help them more. If they could see, Lancaster could see. The sense of solitude and security was deceptive and the vapor amplified some sounds and muted others.

Birds called and squirrels chattered, but they

might have been at his shoulder or a mile away. Will pitched his voice low so it wouldn't carry. "How do you even know where you're going?"

"Compass for a heart," she said, smiling over her shoulder. "And technically I don't know more than our general direction."

A fat black squirrel scampered across a thick tree limb, watching them with obvious interest. "Are black squirrels common here?"

"More common than other places," she replied with a shrug. "Haven't you ever seen one before?"

"Sure." Probably. He didn't typically pay attention to wildlife on a mission. He kept his focus on his target and ignored the things—cover, animals or other people—who got in the way.

Charly crouched suddenly, pressing her fingertips to the soft, dark earth. She held up her other hand, signaling him to stop.

Obediently, he froze in place while she eased forward.

What the hell was she looking at? It couldn't be related to Lancaster and unless he'd lost all his field sense, they were nowhere near where Rich's body might have landed. They'd moved away from that deadly fall just by reaching the cave. Had some scavenger dragged the body this way? He wanted to ask, but refused to interrupt her.

She pressed a finger to her lips and motioned him closer. "Wolf." She pointed to the big paw print near her knee, then to the next one just out of her reach.

"They don't travel alone," he said, mostly to himself.

"No."

"What does that mean for us?"

She stood tall, her gaze tracking up into the trees, then back down. "Stay alert." She smoothed a stray lock of hair back behind her ear.

"You have a theory."

"What makes you say that?"

"I can practically hear the gears turning."

She smiled, but it wasn't an entirely happy expression. "The wolves might have come through, but they're not here right now."

"Please explain that," he said when she stopped.

"All the prey is too happy, too active. If a predator was nearby, the immediate area would be absolutely still, hunkered down and waiting it out."

"Okay, I'll buy that."

Now her grin was quick and sharp. "Remind me to send the government an invoice. Anyway," she continued, "I was really thinking that the wolves might have, um, found an easy meal if the plane went down nearby."

"Oh." Then the full meaning sank in. "Oh," he repeated, imagining a gruesome scenario.

"Apex predators don't turn down easy food if they can get it." She dusted her hands on her pants and set off again.

But now they were both thinking about Clint and how she'd protected his body from a similar fate.

"So the wolves must be somewhere else if the vultures are circling."

"It's a big mountain," she said. "How many on the plane?"

"No idea. I assume it was only the pilot."

"Well, let's get up there and find out." She moved with grace and speed, barely leaving a track along the way. He watched her deliberately choose one step over another without slowing, leaving the wolf prints intact.

"You'd be an excellent teacher," he said, thinking aloud.

"Because I can intimidate as well as track?"

"Something like that."

Her braid flowed down her back when she shook her head.

They stopped long enough to fill up their canteens with fresh water. He was fascinated as she pointed out the different tracks of animals who'd visited recently. "It's been years since I've given any thought to tracking down something other than people," he said.

A smirk curved her lips. "Nature was here first."

"I'm aware. Nature is often part of the briefing…"

"And what? You ignore it?"

"Not exactly. I listen. But it just…doesn't matter. The job has to get done no matter what else is out there." That was simply the way things went in the military. Especially on covert ops. Failure wasn't an option. Clichéd or not, it was a core principle of his service.

"Usually I give any threatening wildlife a wider berth," she said.

"But that's not a choice this time around," he finished for her. "I'll stay alert."

With a nod, she pushed to her feet, her gaze roaming across the cliff they'd just left.

The fog had thinned, but visibility remained limited. The disembodied voices of Lancaster and the mercenaries drifted through the air, accompanied by the occasional sound of an anchor biting into rock.

"I'll be damned," he said, catching a few words that confirmed the men were climbing nearby.

"They're following us straight down the cliff face," she whispered. "Fools."

"Either Lancaster's opposed to more detours, or the guy who fell had something they need."

Charly didn't seem to be listening. She stared into the water as she moved upstream. "Wait a second," she said.

He took a few long strides to catch up. "We have to reach the wreck ahead of them." Ideally, he'd get the key, set a trap for Lancaster, then haul ass off this mountain and let the authorities deal with the mercenaries.

She knelt by the water and swiped a hand across a wet stone, then brought it to her nose. When she turned and held up her fingers, her bright smile made up for the weak sunlight. "It's fuel." She stood, held her hand to his nose. "Take a whiff."

Whatever was on her hand smelled burned to him, as well. "Keep going."

The voices faded behind them, forgotten as they searched swiftly for any evidence of the downed plane. She watched the water; he kept checking the treetops. The damn thing should've left a mark somewhere out here.

He turned back, and his stomach clutched to see the brutal, rocky cliff they'd scaled last night. Intimidating didn't do it justice. Magnificent might've fit, if he hadn't been busy trying not to puke. Ledge or not, they never should've survived that climb in the darkness.

Blind luck? Grace of God? Mother Nature in a benevolent mood? Will gave a mental shout of gratitude to the universe in general.

Unfortunately they were losing the advantage of the fog and would have to take cover or take more fire from Lancaster's men.

"They'll spot us soon," he warned.

"This way," Charly said, pointing to the trees on the facing slope.

When they were safely out of sight, she asked for his binoculars again. He used them first, getting a fix on Lancaster's progress, then gave them to her.

"There." She pointed, held her arm steady while he took a look. "See it?"

Finally, he did. Through the lenses it didn't look like much more than a crumpled ball of paper caught in the rocks. "Could the wreck be downstream? In the water?" If so, Lancaster had regained the advantage.

"I doubt it. If the pilot lost control, that might be the first of a string of pieces that would lead to the crash site."

"Heading downstream."

"Cheer up," she said, with more cheer than the situation called for. "I've heard search and rescue pilots talk."

"So have I." He could imagine well enough a pilot coming over the ridge and cartwheeling out of control. If beacon and key were together, they'd lost any advantage.

"There's no sign of an explosion, so it didn't get blown this direction."

Her excitement, the renewed confidence gleaming in her eyes, roused his curiosity. "What are you getting at?"

"The small-aircraft pilots who fly up here," she explained, "talk about getting tossed and battered by the shifting winds and hard shear all the time."

"Which pushes pilots into this side."

"Yes." Her eyes were bright, eager. "I'm betting the wreck is near the upper tree line and only a bit farther downstream." She punched him lightly on the shoulder. "Lancaster isn't any closer than we are. In fact, we can move faster because it's just you and me. If he refuses to let them detour off the beacon's signal, it will take them longer because of the tougher terrain."

"This is easy terrain?"

"It's all relative," she said with a grin. "Besides, we're younger, more fit, and I'm the area expert. Come on."

Her fresh surge of energy boosted him, too. "Then let's get this done."

He thought she was part mountain goat the

way she scrambled up the slope. His quads burned, and his lungs labored with the quick pace and thin air.

He didn't mind. It was all good and the effort felt like real progress. A couple hours later they hadn't reached the summit, but they had found another piece of the plane, this time part of the landing gear caught up high in a tree.

"That's more like it," he said.

"Yeah, we're getting close," Charly agreed. "And it's recent, so it's probably part of the plane you're after."

"Okay, the compass-for-a-heart thing I've seen firsthand. Last night proved well enough that you know every nook and cranny—literally—around here. But how can you tell how long ago that landed in the tree?"

"Easy. The cracked limbs would be brown and dead if it had hit more than a few days ago. It's still green."

"Of course." It made sense. Surely he would've come to the same conclusion. If he'd thought it mattered. "Have I mentioned lately I'm glad you're on my side?"

She pretended to check her watch. "Right on schedule." Her saucy grin faded. "But a plane could go for miles without that wheel."

He closed his eyes, imagining the rugged mountain trek ahead as miles of gentle, level ground. "In it to win it," he said, sweeping an arm out for her to lead the way.

He told himself he appreciated competent people in any situation. Charly was a friend and despite being attracted, he really should take a step back. For her sake and his.

When this was done, Casey could ship him off to a new assignment in another town. It was how a task force worked. The last thing Will wanted was one more tally in the loss column.

Fellow SEALs and his brother dead, his parents shutting him out—all of that was more than enough to manage. Which was why he didn't dwell on what he couldn't change. Being sad or pissed off didn't bring back the dead, and in his experience it didn't make coping any easier.

Work did that. Movement. Quantifiable progress in the form of successful ops or a cleared to-do list.

Leaving a woman as beautiful and interesting as Charly? No. He had enough common sense to avoid that disaster. He wasn't ready for permanent and she deserved more than temporary.

A few paces ahead of him, he saw the misstep, could only watch as her foot slipped and she landed on her hip. She slid down the slope like a runner into third, using a tree trunk to stop herself.

"Safe," he teased, offering his hand to help her

up. She put her hand in his, and he felt the jolt of awareness. Using him as anchor, she stood and suddenly their joined hands were trapped between their bodies.

Her face tipped up to his, her smiling lips so full and close. Another time, another place, he knew he wouldn't have hesitated. The devilish voice in his head urged him to go for it. "You all right?"

"Sure." Her gaze drifted to his mouth and then back to his eyes. "Slips happen."

Physically, yes. But a slip of the personal variety couldn't be allowed. He plucked a twig from her pack before it could tangle in her hair. "Better keep going."

"Right." She turned, resuming the steep hike with a little more caution.

It reminded him of the way she'd turned her back to him last night. For the first time since his brother's death he wished he wasn't so damned broken.

Chapter Fourteen

Charly stayed on edge the rest of the day, ever alert for the potential danger from the mountain or Lancaster's advance. They'd stopped periodically to check the progress and as she'd anticipated, Lancaster's stubbornness had turned into an advantage for Will's cause.

As if that wasn't enough mental gymnastics, she couldn't keep her mind from wandering back to last night. Kissing Will, she'd felt something unlock. No one had ever made her feel that rush quite that way.

If he hadn't been sensible last night, there would've been no stopping her. She should be grateful. Instead, it was taking a great deal of her energy to stay sensible when she wanted to jump him, to get her hands under those dark clothes and explore every honed inch of him. At this point she didn't care if it ruined the friendship. She knew it would be worth it.

Except it wouldn't be. She respected him—

more, she respected herself. He'd been right; they'd both been running on adrenaline and the thrill of survival. It was challenging enough to keep her mind on the various tasks ahead of her today and they'd only shared a kiss. Mind-blowing, but a kiss.

If they'd had sex, she'd probably be flitting about in a fog of her own making.

Her brain kept dancing through her every personal encounter with him. Hoping to put an end to the merry-go-round of it, she told herself she wouldn't let him talk his way out of another chance should it present itself.

She might not have as much experience as other women her age, but she wasn't an idiot. She knew Will was attracted to her. Knew he felt the chemistry simmering between them. A man just looking to add to his high score didn't take the time Will had taken with her. *Before* they'd hiked into this escalating situation.

"How are you doing?"

His voice lifted the hair at the back of her neck. "Fine." She carefully turned. "Do you need a break?"

Half a grin tilted his mouth up at one corner. "I'm good."

Yeah, she had to agree. With his jacket open and sweat dampening his shirt, molding the fabric to his muscled torso. She told herself the simmer of heat under her skin was an asset against the cooler temperature.

While he checked Lancaster's progress with the binoculars, she indulged in a long, cool drink from her canteen. "Hungry?"

He shrugged. "Sure." He accepted the beef jerky she offered. "Sounds like they've split up."

"What?"

"More radio chatter." He turned the dial and held it where she could hear it, too. "No need for radios if they're together."

"Damn it."

"You said it," he said. "Any ideas?"

Her thoughts scattered for a moment as he tipped his canteen back. A bead of sweat trickled down his neck. Why was that so sexy? Her body temperature climbed. "Keep moving. We have to be getting close."

He nodded as he capped his canteen. "I'll keep the radio on."

When they reached a place where they could walk side by side, she fought the reflex to take his hand. "What will you do when we get there?" she asked, desperate to keep her mind on the bigger issue.

"Assuming we get there first, I'll take control of the device."

"What does it look like?"

"I don't know."

Startled, she looked up at him, hoping he was kidding. The tension in his jaw, his gaze steady and aimed straight ahead, made her realize he was serious. "Great."

"It can't be too big, considering what it does."

"Why would it be on a plane? Seems easier to just have it shipped," she mused.

"Good question."

"Is there anyone with the answer?"

He chuckled, the sound low and deep. "The answer's irrelevant. However it happened, the thing is out here and it's up to me—to us, now—to find it before Lancaster does."

"You aren't curious about the how and why?"

"Only as it relates to my operational success."

"What does that mean?" It sounded irresponsible to her and nothing like the thoughtful, easygoing mailman he'd seemed to be back in Durango.

"Do you ask your customers why they want to take one excursion over another?"

"Sometimes, yes."

He reached down without missing a stride and plucked a fallen twig from the ground. "Bad example." He broke bits of dried bark from the twig as they walked on. "Remember when your parents would say, 'because I said so'?"

"Of course. It's a universal curse."

"Right. Well, there are times when military

ops are simply a matter of pointing a team with a certain skill set at an objective. We take that objective because our commander said so."

"I guess I know that, logically. But it's a tough leap since I knew you first as my mailman."

He smiled down at her. "I know how to think for myself, but during an op what I think takes a backseat to what needs to get done." He flipped her braid. "For the record, I've never done anything on an op or been with a team that took action that I later thought was unnecessary or excessive."

Will watched her from the corner of his eye as she processed that information. A military mind-set didn't appeal to everyone. Not even everyone in the military. Why did he have such an issue with wanting her to understand him? It was dangerous, thinking of her as more than a civilian in harm's way.

Right now, in life-or-death circumstances, was the worst time to let things spiral out of control emotionally or physically. He was about to say as much when the radio crackled.

By tacit agreement, Charly and Will stopped to listen. The bickering was tense and ugly on both sides. Scott's injury was slowing them down and apparently the tracking device was giving them mixed signals.

"Echoes," she explained, then slapped a hand over her mouth as though Lancaster might hear her.

Will had to work hard not to laugh. At both her innocence and the target's unraveling. Impatient, Lancaster had sent Max and James to scout ahead and they'd only managed to get themselves lost.

"The plane's between us," she whispered.

"Or the beacon is."

She curled her lip, clearly unhappy with that reminder. "Let's hurry."

"Won't argue with that."

"We'll make better time if we hike up above the trees."

"But based on what we've found, the crash is down in here with us."

"And heading straight for the beacon is working so well for him."

She had a point. He looked around, as if the plane would suddenly materialize in front of them. "We could be sitting ducks up there," he said, thinking of the sniper they'd had to avoid yesterday.

She planted her hands on her hips. "Trust me?"

"Absolutely."

The word was barely past his lips before she was off like a shot, scrambling for the top of the ridge. Shaking his head, he went after her.

IN THE EVENING, Charly paused just long enough to appreciate a fiery sunset that deserved more than a few seconds of admiration. A day that had started in a soft blur of gray drifted to a close amid broad swipes of orange and purple across the endless sky. Another day, she told herself, with a tall cold beer in one hand, she and Will would have nothing to do but watch the sun kiss the sky good-night.

Tonight, they were racing against the encroaching darkness. If they stopped now and waited until morning, they'd lose the small advantage they'd gained today. She wouldn't let it happen; for Will's op, Clint's honor and her own pride, she was determined to beat Lancaster.

At last they stumbled onto the track of the plane's fatal descent. Together they picked their way over downed limbs and broken trees until they reached the mangled rudder. A few yards ahead, she saw more of the tail and fuselage. Without a flashlight, she couldn't be sure about the wings or cockpit.

"Watch it." Will caught her arm, drew her around a twisted wheel and strut before she tripped. "Let's search what we can without the flashlights."

Through the radio, they'd been keeping tabs on Lancaster's progress. Max and James had been pointed in this direction, and odds were good they'd soon be dealing with unwelcome company.

She'd gotten into the habit of stroking the hilt of the knife sheathed at her hip as they'd hiked out today. Now, with both of them having gone silent, she drew it, mentally daring Max or James to make a move. She had no idea how Will intended to find anything in the dark. Then again, he'd made it clear this wasn't the time for questions—obvious or otherwise.

From down the hill, on the opposite side of the wreck, a beam of light sliced through the shadows and she stilled. Will tapped her shoulder. "Go."

She shook her head, not trusting her voice.

"Let me take this."

She shook her head again.

"Go back to the ridge. I'll find you."

The voices were clearer now, the excitement coming through. Max and James had made good time without the injured Scott and older Lancaster.

"Go."

It wasn't a suggestion—he expected her to follow it like an order. She took a step back as he moved forward. "I'll take your pack." If he was going two against one, or thought he was, he needed to be mobile.

With a frown, he shrugged out of the straps, dropping it silently at her feet.

She had the ridiculous urge to wish him luck, or even kiss him goodbye. Instead, seeing the light of a hunter in his eyes, she eased back into the shadows.

It was harder going with two packs, more of a challenge to move without making a sound, but she managed. Will didn't need to be worrying about her when he was up against two well-armed men who'd proven themselves ruthless.

Part of her wanted him to kill them both, while another part prayed they'd get out of here without being noticed at all.

When she was well back from the wreckage, but not anywhere near the ridge where he wanted her to hide, she looked for a good place to stow the packs. Somewhere they could find them if they had to make a run for it. Not if, *when*, she amended. Whether he took out both of them or not, with Lancaster nearby a hurried escape was inevitable.

Will could complain later, but she wasn't leaving him without some kind of backup. Knife in hand, she crept back down the slope.

Two beams of light roved over the plane and

she knew Will was somewhere at the edge, waiting for his opening.

A loud snap of a boot on debris interrupted Max and James and the men aimed light into the surrounding forest.

If Will had done that it wasn't by mistake.

She tipped her head back and let loose a long wolf howl.

A moment later, a wolf answered her call. Max and James exchanged some harsh words, reaching for weapons or radios. The radio she and Will had taken when they'd left Jeff and Bob at the waterfall was still clipped to Will's belt. Had he remembered to turn it off? She moved closer, ready to leap into the fray if it gave away his position. But gunfire erupted from the trees—from Will—and James and Max hit the ground, searching for cover, too preoccupied to get off a call for help.

She used the commotion to race in behind the mercenaries. *Not the smartest move*, she thought, too late, as it put her on the wrong end of Will's gun, but she stayed put, ready to act.

More lights crisscrossed in the distance. They had only a few minutes before Lancaster and Scott arrived.

The options were too few. She felt around in the dark until she found a pinecone. Not a great weapon, but a decent distraction. She jumped up and hurled it at Max. It found its mark in the middle of his back. She crouched behind a tree as one of the men charged her direction. "Will, run!" she shouted. "The others are nearly here."

"You first," he called back.

Guns growled as bullets flew between Will and the one mercenary. She had to move or she'd be caught for sure on the wrong side of the crash site.

"Charly?" James was nearly on top of her, but he was looking high, instead of low. "Come on now. We can come to terms."

She knew his terms. Breath held, gauging her options and dwindling time, she listened, eyes closed.

One more step. Come on, one more.

Finally, he moved, and she drove her elbow into his knee, then jumped up and punched him square in the throat. Leaving him choking, she ran for her life to where she'd left the packs. It sounded like a war zone behind her. The only good news was that the chaos would keep any wildlife at bay for a while.

She hitched her pack on her shoulders, praying Will would show up. Hearing boots, she spun around, knife swinging.

"Easy." Will caught her arm with quiet authority. "It's me."

She flared her free hand, unwilling to drop

the knife. He let her go in favor of picking up his pack. They moved farther into the trees before Will stopped her.

"Too close," she said.

"We won't stay long." He pulled her down beside him. "Are you hurt?"

"No. You?"

"I'm fine."

"Then let's move. They'll find us here."

Will shook his head. "They're too distracted." But the four men were already searching around the plane, trying to get organized.

She wanted more space. Now.

"Did you kill James?"

She shook her head, trying to slow the panicked beat of her heart.

"Oh. Here he comes."

She saw him stagger out, joining the others in a circle of gathered flashlights. The angry voices carried up to their position.

"Hunt them down!"

"You let them get away?"

That was probably Scott, but it was impossible to tell which man had shouted amid all the raised voices. Charly wanted to cover her ears, wanted to shut it all out. The tension rolled off the mercenaries in waves as the arguing and accusations were hurled back and forth.

Will's hand, warm on her shoulder, was the

only thing keeping her from bolting. Irrational, but true—her flight reaction had her by the throat and wasn't letting go. Suddenly a gunshot rang out across the mountain, sending birds that had recently settled for the night into a swirl of panic and feathers flitting across the dark sky.

She, too, jerked in response, but Will had gathered her close. His strong arms were the only security, his embrace the beginning and end of her world. She clung to him, smothering her urge to scream against his warm chest. They were still too close. Any sound and they, too, would be dead tonight.

"You can't leave him there," Scott said.

"Watch me," Lancaster replied.

She couldn't look, but she heard the sounds, the smack and thud as punches were thrown. She hated the senseless killing and violence. Nothing was worth this. No one deserved Lancaster's blatant disregard for life. She wondered if she'd ever find her temper through the icy fist of dread clamped around her heart.

"It's too close to the wreck. The guide talked about predators."

"I don't give a damn. The pilot's dead. What's one more body? We'll be gone by first light."

"You're inviting trouble."

"You have your orders. Track them down."

"Impossible in the dark," Scott argued. "We'll camp here. Protect the site."

"Go find them!" Lancaster shouted. "Now."

Another hard smack, then someone was spitting, choking. "We can't track them in the dark. We don't know who's helping her, just that he has skills."

"I hired you for your skills! We aren't leaving witnesses."

"One thing we agree on," Scott declared with a threatening finality that chilled her. "I'll take care of it in the morning. We camp here. Get rid of the body."

"No." Lancaster sounded like a petulant child. "You shot him, you get rid of him."

Will gave her a gentle squeeze. "Is there anywhere to hide up here?" he whispered against her ear.

With a nod, she pushed back. Moving carefully so they wouldn't draw Lancaster's attention, she led them back to the safety of the ridge.

Chapter Fifteen

Will wasn't sure how she'd done it, but she'd gotten them away safely, unerringly finding their packs as they retreated from the crash site with no more than the moonlight to show the way. He had to admit her skills were more than a little eerie. She moved with absolute silence when she wanted to. He knew damn well if it hadn't been for her khaki pants he would've lost her.

"I've said it before, but I'm glad you're on my side," he said, walking deeper into the shelter. He dropped his pack against the back wall of the small cave she'd found.

"Same goes," she said, her voice catching.

He wanted to soothe, but exhaustion and adrenaline left him searching for the right words. "Thanks for not listening to me."

"Sure." She continued to stare into the dark, eyes wide, searching for Lancaster's next inevitable attack.

He put his arm around her, squeezed her shoulder. "You made those wolf calls, right?"

"One of them," she admitted, rubbing her hands over her arms. "The first one."

The woman he'd thought could never break was about to shatter. He had to do something. Anything. The world outside the cave started to come to life again. Small things rustled. A sound similar to her wolf call rose into the sky.

"Is that one looking for you?"

"No. He knows a fraud when he hears it."

She'd sounded pretty genuine to him. A sudden screech split the air, making him jump. "Christ, that's loud."

"Screech owl," she whispered, hugging herself. "Worse when it bounces off the rocks."

He had to work, but he got her pack off her shoulders, set it beside his as the owl cried out again. "Will it go on all night?"

"So what if it does? It can't hurt you."

"It can sure as hell keep me awake."

"You sound like *My Cousin Vinnie*."

He turned. "What?"

"The movie? The city-boy lawyer trying to cope with the differences of a small town in the Deep South."

"I know the movie." She was starting to sound closer to normal, but she wasn't there quite yet. "I'll start a fire."

"That'll lead them right back to us."

"I don't think so." He patted his gun. "But they're welcome to try. We've got solid rock at our back, which leaves them only one approach. I guarantee I'll shoot first, and I don't miss."

"Fine."

He figured the chill gripping her from head to toe had more to do with her easy agreement than his weapons expertise.

When he had a small fire going, he came back for her. "See anything?"

"Not yet. What if they see the fire?"

"It'll be okay."

She turned, and his heart clutched at the pain in her midnight eyes. "He shot James. Because of me."

"No. James died because he signed on to work for a crazy man." He gathered her into his arms, helpless to do anything else. "It's not your fault." She didn't cry, but tremors ripped through her frame, pain and anxiety determined to find a way out. "Lancaster's gone off the edge."

"Not the right one," she said after a minute.

He choked back a laugh. "He won't get away with it, I promise." He ran his hand up and down her back.

"I believe you." Her breath quieted, and her heartbeat wasn't as wild against his chest. "I want to help you take him down."

"That's good. I'll need you."

She wriggled in his embrace, pressed a kiss to his cheek, then stepped back. "Okay. Let's make a plan."

"Sure." He was glad she'd turned the corner, but a manic rush of energy with no safe direction could be as problematic as the brittle shock. "But let's settle down for a minute first." He handed her a canteen.

She took a long drink, swiped her hand across her mouth. Then she shrugged out of her jacket. "I'm antsy."

"It happens."

She rooted through her pack, making a happy sound when she found some sort of wipes she used to clean away remnants of the day. "Want one?"

He accepted with a smile, started thinking about what they had left to eat. It was better than thinking about suffering another night alone with her in tight quarters. Another night when he couldn't touch her like he wanted to.

"Will?"

He turned, nearly bumping into her.

Charly looked up at him. She wanted to take a bite out of that square, beard-stubbled jaw more than she wanted another meal of granola bars and beef jerky. But it was clear he was expecting her to break apart at any moment. He was probably right. Part of her still felt shaky, but for increasingly different reasons than shock and death. She knew she should wait until they were done here. Until they had some time off the mountain to see how they felt about each other when life was normal again.

Should sucked.

But they shared the meal, and she gave a valiant effort to diverting her thoughts away from jumping Will's hard body. "We should talk," she said.

"About?"

"Anything."

He gave her a wary look over the top of the canteen. "Tell me about your first solo hike."

"No." She reached down and loosened her boot laces. "Something else."

He shifted his feet. "Okay." He pointed to his chin. "See this scar?"

"Mmm-hmm." She wanted to kiss it. Along with any others she could find.

"Happened when I was eight. Nine? No, eight, because—"

He went quiet when her hands gripped his hips. "Will?"

"Wh-what?"

"I'm done talking about the past."

"You are?"

She nodded. "Let's talk about right now." She

trailed her fingers up over his chest. "I want you." She had to clear her throat, but she pressed on, determined to get the words out. "I want you to make love with me. Here. Tonight. Tomorrow doesn't matter. Might be too late."

"Charly, what you're feeling, it's just a basic reaction—"

"Stop. We both know this isn't 'just' anything." She pulled her braid over her shoulder, started combing it out with her fingers. "Do you want me, Will?"

His answer was to grab her with greedy hands, jerking her right up against his hard body. She had a split second to gasp before his mouth found hers. Claimed her. The heat of it rolled through her, sizzled and popped like sparklers.

She clutched his shoulders, straining for balance as his tongue swept into her mouth, one sensuous velvet stroke after another. Her body was primed and ready for him instantly. She felt as if she'd been ready for him her entire life. Pushing layers of fabric out of the way, she sighed in delight when her hands found warm skin at last.

He broke the kiss only long enough to strip off his jacket and shirt, then push away the barrier of hers. The firelight danced, highlighting acres of sculpted muscle. A better view than she'd imagined.

Amazed, hardly believing her eyes, she reached out, trailing her fingertips across his pecs, down the washboard abs. He was stunning and she was…

"Stunning."

She blinked. That had been her thought, but Will's voice. Aimed at her. She didn't want to call him a liar, but in her opinion the simple cotton bra—her entire body—was better defined as serviceable.

"Not too late for second thoughts." He tipped her chin up and she had to close her eyes or meet his gaze. "Do you want me to stop?"

No coward, she stared into his blue eyes, burning hot. For her. It was astounding. In all her fantasies, and her rare real encounters, no man had looked at her quite the way Will did now. "No second thoughts here."

His smile was a wicked flash before he leaned in and took her mouth once more. Kisses over her jaw, down her throat. The rough whiskers on his jaw scraped her skin as he nipped at the sensitive curve of her shoulder. She gasped as his hands cruised over her breasts, thumbs slipping behind the thin cotton to tease her nipples.

With a flick, her bra was undone and tossed aside. She couldn't find the energy to care as his mouth replaced his hands on first one breast and then the other. Running her fingers through his hair, arching into his lavish attention had her nearing a climax already.

She reached for his waistband, carefully opening the button fly around his erection. His breath shuddered across her skin when she closed her hand around him. She tingled, inside and out, as sensation layered over sensation while he learned what her body craved.

Him.

He laid her back on the sleeping bag as if she was the most exquisite treasure in his world.

And when he rose over her and drove into her with one swift thrust, she felt treasured, even as a sudden climax ripped through her. She reached for him, stroking everything she could reach. His broad back, his narrow hips, his biceps and shoulders strong as iron. Even that tiny scar he'd gotten when he was eight. Or nine. With her whole body she embraced him, drew him in and held as his rhythm seduced her, carried her up toward another peak.

Had anything ever felt as good?

Never. She wanted it to go on and on, felt as though it did as his body went taut on that final bolt of pleasure. Still intimately joined, he brushed her nose with his, then kissed her with such tenderness, she shivered beneath him.

He braced on one elbow. "Cold?"

"No. Probably never again." She kissed his chin.

"But you have goose bumps," he teased, his teeth scraping gently over her shoulder.

She caressed his calf with her toes. "Whose fault is that, I wonder."

He rolled to his side, tucking her close and wrapping himself around her. "Sleep. I'll take the first watch."

"All right." She smiled into the banked fire. If he felt half as good as she did right now they were most likely invincible.

Chapter Sixteen

Will came awake suddenly, blinking to make sense of the near dark around him. He was alone under the sleeping bag and the sun wasn't more than a vague rumor in the sky beyond their shelter. That made two days running that Charly had managed to wake before him. How did she do that?

Though she moved silently, he knew her absence had been the distraction that pulled him from sleep. It wasn't the most comfortable self-realization. As a rule, he didn't actually sleep with the women who'd shared his bed. Or sleeping bag, as was the case here.

He sat up and smiled, watching her braid all of that silky midnight hair. Just hours ago he'd had all that in his hands. His body heated, recalling the feel of it sliding over his skin.

Their clothes were a mess and the closest thing they had to a shower was an ice-cold stream somewhere in the distance. Yet, wardrobe malfunctions aside, he wasn't sure he'd ever seen a woman as beautiful as Charly.

Knowing her had changed him. Made him want more than he could have. More than her body, he wanted to be the man she needed. However things went with Lancaster today, he knew he wasn't the same man he'd been when he'd arrived in Durango.

"Going to laze around here all day?" She cast a look at him over her shoulder.

"I wish." His easy, instinctive answer surprised him. He decided to roll with it. They could get serious later. "When this is over, we need to come back up here."

She bowed her head a moment, then shifted around to face him. When she met his gaze, he noticed the sheen of tears in her eyes, but her voice was steady. "To banish this entire Lancaster debacle and reclaim this area as a more positive experience."

He nodded and reached for her hand, lacing their fingers. She had such strength in her hands. "Capturing Lancaster is step one, honoring Clint step two. But I don't want you standing at your shop and looking up here only to have that view haunted by dread or pain."

"I know bad things happen, no matter what or who caused them."

"You also know living is more than just surviving the bad things."

She blinked several times, and her eyes, clear now, locked with his. Leaning closer, she brushed her lips lightly across his cheek and then his mouth. "You are a thoughtful man, Will Chase."

She kissed him again and he let her, sinking into the kind, if overblown, compliment she offered. "It's a gift," he murmured against her warm skin, more than willing to change the subject.

"*You* are a gift," she corrected gently. "We should make time to visit the places that haunt you, too."

He froze, uncertain how to interpret that. Yes, he wanted her, but it was hard to believe she really wanted to be with him beyond this misadventure. No intelligent woman would. Not after the things he'd told her. The list was too long and, aside from his parents' home, the places that haunted him were on the other side of the world or locked in vaults in the dark corners of his mind.

"Strange as all this has been, we made some positive memories last night," she said.

"Agreed." He drew her close, wrapping her in his arms, trying to chase away the awkwardness he'd introduced. This perfect moment would be enough. For now, and for later when she came to her senses. If they didn't get another chance at this, he wanted her to know what he felt for her. He wanted her to know she was unique, precious, and any man would be lucky to have her.

It just couldn't be him. He didn't want to burden her with his baggage. When this was over, he'd explain that so she understood.

"It's three against two today."

"Almost seems unfair. To them," she said as she cinched her bootlaces.

She humbled him with her unwavering confidence. Knowing her skills and unflappable composure, it meant that much more.

He could almost hear the echo across the mountain as his heart dropped into her hands. Knowing men fell in love didn't mean he'd ever thought he'd be one of them. "Let's get back to the crash site," he said. Later was soon enough to deal with the emotions churning in his gut where Charly was concerned.

An hour later, when they arrived at the crash site, he saw they were too late. Will reached for his knife as Scott, Max and Lancaster crawled through the wreckage, searching for Lancaster's life's work.

He wasn't surprised that the scene looked worse in daylight. The fuselage was cracked open like an egg. Sharp scents of fuel and oil spoiled the clear air. The wings were stubs, sheared by the trees, and the tail was absent, but Lancaster's presence was enough confirmation they were at the right site. Debris, like the first piece they'd found, was tangled randomly in the branches above and behind them. From above, Will imagined the crash site looked something like a poorly executed fire break. Will pulled out his phone and took pictures, wishing there was a cell tower to send them to Casey. If Lancaster had been able to get a helicopter up here, he would've gotten away with the Blackout Key too easily. Finally, a reason to appreciate high altitude and technology-free wilderness.

Despite their focus, by accident or design the men were positioned in a way that prevented a surprise attack. He couldn't take all three of them without a diversion. His best diversion was Charly, but using her as bait put a bad taste in his mouth.

"Some mess," he whispered to Charly.

"Where's a flare when you need one?" she murmured, her gaze on the scene, obviously not caring any more than he did about the fate of Lancaster and his two remaining mercenaries.

Will pictured his limited options. Action, reaction. Cause, effect.

"I can go in," Charly said.

"No." He didn't care that it was the right call.

"Bogus radio call?" She held up the radio.

He shook his head.

"Don't leave me out of it," she said through gritted teeth.

"Not that, either." He rubbed her shoulder, pressed his lips to her temple. "First we need to know he found the key."

She nodded, making an okay sign with her fingers.

When Lancaster found the key, Will would be able to make a final decision about how to contain the men and the device.

He signaled to Charly and they retreated back into the thicker cover of the trees. "What's his best route out of here?"

"It's only a few hours on foot from here to another park access point by way of a cleared and well-marked trail."

"Then how much longer to Durango?"

"Not long at all if he has a car there."

"He won't go back over the mountain?"

"Would you want to go back the way we came?"

Will shook his head, suppressing his smile. "Just making sure there isn't a direct route."

"He'll make better time going down and taking the road."

"Does he know that?"

She grimaced. "I gave each of them standard trail guide maps for reference when we started out. But I'm not sure he knows where the trail is from here."

Will considered what they'd seen and heard. Lancaster had been furious about the shifting timeline and ongoing delays, natural and man-made, keeping him from the Blackout Key and his revenge. He was coming unhinged, had lost all but two men in the search. There had to be a way to turn that into an advantage.

A plan took shape in Will's mind. If—when—Lancaster found the damned key, this could all be over by the end of the day. He focused on that critical detail.

Yet Will knew that when Lancaster was in custody and the key safely out of commission, he'd face a new crossroads with Charly. *One thing at a time*, he coached himself, hearing the team leader's voice from his first operation as a SEAL.

"What's wrong?" she asked, worry weighting her tone.

"Nothing. Unless the key isn't there."

"Right. But I can see the wheels turning," she said, repeating his words to her last night. "Tell me the plan."

"Our best option is to move around, cut off

the logical egress from the crash site. He knows he needs to go downhill."

"All right," she said on a quiet chuckle. "Where do you want me?"

"Behind me," he said, ignoring the way her gaze narrowed. "After I send a specific emergency message over the radio."

"They could hear that."

"They don't know we have a working radio," he reminded her. "With the right phrase my message should bring reinforcements and not alert Lancaster." He hoped Casey had mobilized men into the Four Corners area after their last conversation—it would make the chain of custody cleaner. Either way, Lancaster was going down today.

"Do you want me to take Scott or Max?"

Neither. But that wasn't an answer she'd accept. "Max." The man who'd carried the tracking device from the start was tired, irritable and the closest to Charly's size. "Keep him alive if possible."

Her dark brows rose. "If?"

He nodded. "This is life or death. All three of those men are desperate. Hopefully it won't get that bad, but just in case, you're my priority."

"I am?"

He took a long breath. "I want you to live

more than I want him alive to testify against Scott and Lancaster."

Her smile rivaled the sun. "Same goes." She pressed up on her toes and kissed him. "Assuming someone is smart enough to give you a medal or some kind of award for this, I want you to be alive to receive it."

"It's a deal."

They stayed low and moved quickly, both of them listening for any sounds of progress from Lancaster. The random shouts didn't sound good, and Will wasn't sure what that meant for his chance of success. He didn't see how it was possible that someone had found the crash site and robbed Lancaster of his prize.

But if the key had never been on the plane... He stopped that thought before it could gain momentum and cloud his analysis.

He paused when he got his first head-on look at the cockpit of the small aircraft. Burrowed into the scorched earth, sparkling as the sunlight danced on shattered glass, the pilot was slumped lifeless against the instrument panel.

Will halted when Lancaster's rambling suddenly ceased. Hearing the victorious shout, he knew he had to act. From here, the solution wasn't perfect, but all three men would be in front of him. Drawing his handgun, he stood tall and entered the clearing created by the downed plane.

With Charly at his back, he moved forward, confident he had the upper hand. "Arms up," he called. The three men stopped moving, but didn't comply. "Arms up," he repeated. "And drop the weapons. Reed Lancaster, your little field trip is over."

"Take them out," Lancaster ordered Scott and Max.

Will saw the hesitation in each man's face, knew they were weighing the odds. "Let Charly take your weapons." He gave her a nod, and she moved toward Max.

"You're outnumbered," Lancaster declared with absolute hatred in his eyes. "Do something," he barked at Scott. "Take them out!"

Will kept his gaze on Scott and Lancaster while Charly skirted the edge of his peripheral vision on her way to take care of Max. "Get real already," he said. "You can't win."

"Who the hell are you?"

Will kept his gun on Lancaster while he answered Scott. "Private contractor, just like you."

Scott vented his disbelief, and Lancaster bellowed as he raised his gun and fired.

The software genius had lousy aim. Will charged forward, furious and tired of this jackass. Two against one didn't bother him, not when he saw Charly holding her own against Max. He tackled Lancaster with all of his pent-up frustration, taking him down. The fumes from the crash rose up, choking him, but he ignored it.

Beneath him, Lancaster gagged, and Will knew that any second now Scott would land on him, or shoot him to protect his profit. He landed a solid punch and flipped Lancaster, using him as a shield against Scott. The older man landed a few punches with a force driven by madness, but Will fought back with knees, elbows and fists.

Until Lancaster was suddenly hauled off him and Charly's voice cut through the blood rushing through his head.

"I'm sorry," she said.

"Surrender or we shoot," Scott said.

Will looked up, blinking. Max and Scott had guns leveled on her. One at her head, one at her belly. He considered bluffing about backup, or that she didn't mean anything, but it was too late for that. He wasn't close enough for a rapid strike.

Defeated, he held up his hands. "You win."

CHARLY SCOLDED HERSELF. She'd disarmed Max, had him where she wanted him, and let herself get distracted when Lancaster took a shot at Will. That split second of panic and she'd lost her footing on the muddy ground surrounding the plane. Her mistake had distracted Will and now they were both propped against trees, hands cuffed at the wrist with zip ties, under the armed guard of Max and Scott.

"I have what I came for." Lancaster dropped to one knee too close to her face. He held up a black plastic box not much bigger than a deck of cards, then tucked it into his pocket.

"So take it and get off my mountain." She couldn't believe how much blood had been spilled for that unexceptional device.

"With pleasure," Lancaster said. With the unyielding tree at her back, there was no escaping his sour breath. She tried not to inhale. "If you get me off this damned mountain in one piece I might let you both live."

She had to give him points for the honest disclaimer. *Might* was a slim chance at life. And a slim chance was better than already dead. It felt like a lousy variation on the rock-paper-scissors game.

"I'll help you." She didn't look at Will. Couldn't risk taking her eyes off Lancaster. Right now Lancaster only knew they were working together. While he was obsessed with his device, she didn't want him to gain any advantage. If he recognized how far she'd go to protect Will, Lancaster would use her love as leverage.

Love. Charly closed her eyes as it washed over

her. The feeling was impractical at best and the relationship—if running around a mountain counted as such—couldn't possibly survive. Still, if these were her final hours, she wouldn't live them in denial. Having seen Will in action, she knew the odds Lancaster found favorable—three armed men against a restrained man and woman—were only an illusion.

She opened her eyes. "Where do you want to go?"

"Durango."

"Do you realize what you're asking?"

Lancaster stared, his expression blank. "Enlighten me."

She suppressed the shiver as fear trickled down her spine. "You can't go back the way we came."

"Why not?"

She stared him right in the eye. "We've radioed park rangers and left a trail of bread crumbs." The lie, boosted with a grain of truth since they'd set up Jeff and Bob to be rescued, must have been convincing.

"You bitch." He backhanded her, bouncing her head off the tree. Her vision blurred until there were two of everything. She could only hope she was focusing on the real version of Lancaster.

"Tell me how to get off this mountain or you die right here."

"Fine." She tasted blood where her teeth had torn the inside of her cheek. "You're better off taking the cleared trail on this side of the mountain and hiring a car to get you out of Colorado." There wouldn't be any safe place for him, not anywhere in the world, with Will on his tail. With luck, they could gain the upper hand along the way to the trailhead.

Lancaster cut the straps holding her to the tree and it shamed her when she slumped forward, still reeling from the blow. He hauled her to her feet by her bound hands. "Any tricks and I'll take my chances on my own."

"No tricks," she promised as they formed up. "But it's fine with me if you leave us here."

"Shut up and lead." Scott's rifle bit into her low back, pushing her forward.

"Just a second." She stumbled, heard Will's deep voice, but couldn't make out the words. Something was wrong, but the cause eluded her. "One second," she said again, from her knees. She peered out at the world, but it seemed as though she was watching the forest through a narrowing telescope. A flash of heat speared up to her head as a ring of darkness closed in. Her stomach twisted, and she battled the nausea. She was passing out. God knew what they'd do to her and Will if she couldn't function as a guide.

Deep male voices locked in a furious debate

surrounded her, though the words were incomprehensible. It made the beckoning quiet all the more tempting. So tempting to give in, to be done with this entire problem.

Only the thought of Will's fate kept her from giving in. She thought of her grandmother's stories of ancient days. A time of honorable warriors and mystical shamans. She knew this land inside and out, body and soul.

"Water," she rasped, but no one seemed to hear.

She felt the cool, moist floor of the forest against her battered cheek. Her mind drifted like a feather on the wind, searching for a tether, a reason to land. *Will*. Will needed her. She sensed it and struggled against the pain reeling behind her eyes.

"Water," she said again, pushing herself upright, forcing her eyes open.

Someone echoed the command a moment before a canteen was placed to her lips. She sputtered and coughed, but it helped.

"More."

"No." Lancaster's denial didn't surprise her. "Can you see?"

"Well enough." Maybe. She didn't need to. This was the land of her ancestors. She could walk out of here blind if she had to. Though she hoped it didn't come to that. "One more sip. Please?"

"She'll lead us off a cliff," Max grumbled. "Give her the canteen."

The hard aluminum banged into her hands, and she managed to grip it before it fell to the ground. "Thank you," she said after another small drink. It helped to rinse the taste of blood from her mouth.

She closed her eyes, found her bearings and turned west. "This way."

"We should kill them and go," Scott said from a few paces behind her.

"Yeah, because that's worked so well," Max replied. "Four men are already dead because of this mountain."

"We can't let them live."

The announcement barely fazed her. Charly knew Scott was right. Witnesses were not part of the equation for the mercenaries. She wondered if Scott and Max realized Lancaster wouldn't leave them alive, either.

It wasn't her problem. At least not as long as she was breathing. She would lead and trust Will to figure a way out of his restraints as well as this nightmare.

Chapter Seventeen

Will ambled on with the group, his hands tied behind his back, his weapons confiscated. Max had his knife and the radio; Scott had taken his handgun. Standard protocol and really, not problematic in the long run. He could take all three of these class-A jerks with his hands behind his back. And he would. Just as soon as Charly was clear.

It wasn't over, but getting captured wouldn't qualify this as his finest hour.

There was still a knot in his gut from Charly's collapse. Watching her, he knew she wasn't fully recovered—her left foot was dragging a bit, and no matter how they prodded her, she couldn't keep up a quick pace for more than a few minutes.

At this point, he wasn't sure she could even find the trail if it was lit with neon lights and a parade of forest animals waving signs. They hiked across relatively easy terrain under a heavy cloud of silence. He wouldn't make his move until he was sure she could get clear on her own. Or until they were out of time.

He had to believe his distress call had been heard by the tech-savvy specialists assigned to support this op by Director Casey. Regardless, he would be sure no one left this mountain with the Blackout Key. It was hard to comprehend how an unassuming black plastic block, small enough to fit into his palm, could be the nation's undoing.

The damned thing didn't look dangerous. He supposed it had been purposely designed to resemble a benign external hard drive.

"How does it work, anyway?" he asked as they crossed an open field. The grass was dormant now and small patches of crisp white snow dotted the area here and there. He imagined Charly had seen this field in every season, would know every plant, animal and stone. Remembering their earlier conversation, he decided he'd ask her about it when they were safe again. His mind played tricks on him, imagining what it would be like to kiss her here in each one of those seasons.

"Not your business," Max replied, pulling him back to the task at hand.

"Which means you don't know."

"I know you should shut up before I slap tape across your mouth."

"Seems like a lot of effort and a big waste of life to me." He wanted to provoke Lancaster. Casey wanted solid intel as to which pieces of Lancaster's grand scheme for revenge were already in place. "Now you can make your statement, is that it, Lancaster?"

"Shut him up," Scott grumbled.

"That little doohickey will show the billionaires who should be boss, right?" *Here we go,* Will thought as Lancaster abruptly turned on his heel and stalked back, a ferocious scowl on his face.

"This 'doohickey' can wipe your bank account in minutes. It will show the corporate mongers that they can't steal from the innovators." He shook the black square in Will's face. "My design, my creation will put the power where it belongs."

Power to the crazies. Not a great global policy.

"I was robbed," Lancaster continued in a calmer voice, "my career and reputation destroyed."

Will didn't see how kidnapping and murder would rectify anything, but he kept quiet.

"This device is literally the key to the kingdom that should have been mine a lifetime ago."

"You sure can hold a grudge."

"What I hold," he said, voice rising once more, "is justice. They will pay. One man, one program, one company at a time."

The man had mastered dramatic flair. Will might've laughed in his face, had Lancaster been less insane. "Were you ever in the theater? When you weren't working on the doohickey, that is."

"Imbecile." With that declaration, Lancaster left Will and Max to bring up the rear of the column as Charly guided them through a thick stand of trees. The trail couldn't be too far. When they got there, Lancaster wouldn't need hostages anymore.

"How much farther, Charly?"

"Don't answer that," Lancaster barked. "No more talking."

"You'll kill me anyway. I'll talk if I want to," Will muttered. "Hey, Charly, are there any snakes around here?"

"You're obnoxious," Max said, smacking the back of Will's head.

"It's a valid concern." He should have insisted the two of them create a code phrase, but he'd been distracted by the woman as much as by outliving Lancaster.

"Stick to the clear areas and it won't be a problem," she called over her shoulder, against Lancaster's wishes.

"Just shoot him now," Scott ordered. "Better to dump the body up here than closer to the trail."

Charly stopped and faced Lancaster. "You said you'd let us go."

"He's a problem."

"You're the problem," she snapped.

"That's hardly a rational argument," Lancaster replied. "I'm surrounded by idiots. Can you keep him quiet?"

Will met her pleading gaze, saw her shoulders go stiff. "Hush," she said without any heat.

"Last chance," Lancaster said to Will. To Charly, he gave a nod. "Go."

Scott jerked his chin at Max, and Will braced for the inevitable. With plenty of cover here for Charly to use for an escape, he decided to let them try and take him out.

Max kicked the back of Will's knees, sending him to the ground. Instead of sprawling, Will tucked and rolled, using the momentum to barrel into Scott. The mercenary leader went headlong into a tree trunk, knocking himself out.

Shouts and oaths bounced off the trees. Will scrambled for cover as Max started shooting.

"Will!"

"Run, Charly!" He caught the flash of color as Charly bolted out of sight. Smart. Let him handle this.

Max came at him, gun drawn. Will jumped to his feet, daring the mercenary to fire. Max bobbled the weapon, eyes going wide as Will charged him and the shot went high.

He planted a bone-crushing roundhouse kick into Max's ribs and the mercenary fell to his knees, wheezing.

A scream split the air, and Will jerked in that direction, praying Charly wasn't the source.

He quickly pinned Max to the ground, his boot on the man's throat. "Surrender or die."

Max spread his hands away from his body. Whatever words he was trying to utter around Will's boot sounded cooperative enough.

Will eased back, just enough so Max could catch his breath.

Looking around, he saw Scott still unconscious and no sign of Charly or Lancaster. He maneuvered until his hands were in front of him. "Cut me loose," he ordered. "Try anything and I'll kill you."

Max resembled a deer caught in the headlights of an oncoming truck.

"Use my knife. Slowly." When he was free, Will rubbed his wrists, then planted a knockout punch to Max's jaw. Dragging Max over to join Scott, he reclaimed his weapons and seized their packs and the weapons they'd brought in.

Binding the men together back to back, he left them next to the tree.

"Charly?"

The complete lack of a reply turned the trickle of sweat between his shoulder blades to icy trepidation. Pausing every few steps to listen, he circled the area. No sign of her or Lancaster. Will resumed the route she'd been on, certain he'd find her right away.

He didn't.

Crap.

Lancaster wouldn't go down without a fight, but Charly was a scrapper fueled with determination to live. What did the persistent silence mean? It crawled under his skin, making him uneasy.

He looked up, watching the trees for the clues Charly had taught him. Nothing moved. Not a curious squirrel or scolding bird. Everything had taken cover, hiding from the loud humans. Everything.

Charly would've done the same. Moving with caution, ready and eager to combat any strike, he stepped, listened and stepped again. If Lancaster had found her or killed her, he'd be gloating or barreling down the mountain in an attempt to outrun Will.

And if Charly had subdued Lancaster, she wouldn't be hiding.

Damn it. If the roles were reversed, Charly would've spotted him by now. She'd be working her way around to help him out. He couldn't let his mind drift, couldn't afford the negativity of comparing his skills to hers. He might not know every inch of this particular landscape, but he knew his personal strengths.

He backtracked to where he'd left the gear he'd taken from Scott and Max. Picking up a radio, he double clicked twice, the signal he'd seen Scott use to get Lancaster's attention.

"Hold," came the whispered reply.

Will repeated the signal.

This time the single word, packed full of irritation, was accompanied by the hoot of an owl. He might not know exactly which type of owl she'd mimicked but he knew any owl worth the name was sound asleep this time of day.

Will smiled to himself and waited. She made the call once more and it was enough to give him a direction.

In a perfect world he'd pinch Lancaster between Charly and himself. He wasn't sure they had that much luck left. His knife in hand, the long blade back against his forearm, he advanced, using the trees as cover.

Finally, he caught a glimpse of Lancaster's sleeve. The man was crouched low behind a tree. Tired of playing cat and mouse with this jerk, Will was tempted to throw the knife and be done.

The required explanation and apology he'd owe Director Casey flitted through his mind. The nation supposedly needed the man alive. Resigned, Will ignored temptation and stuck with procedure, silently creeping closer to the target.

He recognized the jacket was a trap a moment too late—the blow landed hard across his shoulders. Lancaster followed up the surprise attack with a heavy branch he brandished like a baseball bat.

Dodging and ducking, Will's feet slipped on the forest floor as he blocked the vicious swings. He gripped the knife, but couldn't get close enough to use it. Couldn't get clear enough to throw it.

The radio at his belt crackled with voices, but the words were garbled, his mind fully occupied with his battle for survival. "Go for help," he hollered, not even knowing if Charly could hear him. He had to buy her enough time to escape. To live.

Will knew hand-to-hand combat. He faced Lancaster as he would an angry bear and stayed alert of his surroundings so he wouldn't run out of room. His fighting sense had been honed to a razor-sharp edge, and he knew how to learn from every engagement. There were solutions, even when fighting a man mad with desperation. Will's real disadvantage was keeping said madman alive.

On a pained shriek, Lancaster suddenly went down, his white-knuckled hands still locked around the branch. He rolled to his side, and Will saw a knife, the hilt decorated with a mosaic turquoise feather, protruding from the man's calf. Over the fallen man, Will met Charly's enigmatic dark eyes. "Nice throw."

"You had him," she said. "I just got impatient."

He nodded, winked. "There are times when patience is overrated."

A smile bloomed across her face, and his heart tripped a little as it recovered from the fight.

"The owl call was a nice touch."

"I thought the same about the radio. He was almost on me at that point."

Will marched up to Lancaster and yanked the branch from his hands. "You are done."

"Who *are* you?"

"Just your average mailman," Will said, grinning at Charly. "You called in the troops, right?"

"Yes. But we're better off if we can meet them on the trail."

"Then that's what we'll do." He flipped Lancaster to his belly and secured the man's hands. A pat down for the Blackout Key came up empty. "Where's the key?"

"I lost it," Lancaster said.

"Not buying it." He tipped his head to Charly, and she went to search Lancaster's jacket. "Not here," she called, kicking around the debris at the base of the tree.

Will studied Lancaster for a long moment. The dirt-smeared face and cold eyes remained smug. Even now, the man thought he could win, thought he had some play left. Will reached for the ammo holder still clipped to Lancaster's belt. The older man grimaced and swore.

Opening the compartment, Will found the device. "Jackpot." He patted Lancaster's cheek. "Thanks." Standing, he pocketed the device that had the attention of the nation's elite security agencies.

He pulled the knife from Lancaster's leg and cleaned the blade on his pants before handing it back to Charly.

"He can walk, but we should dress that before we move out," she said.

Will didn't want to do anything to assist Lancaster. The man had put them through a crucible on his selfish quest for vengeance. "Can you hold him while I go back for the other two and the packs?"

She tossed her knife from hand to hand, a wicked gleam in her midnight eyes. "No problem."

He jogged back to where he'd left Scott and Max. Taking only the weapons, he forced the other two to haul what remained of the packs. They wouldn't quite leave the forest as they'd found it, but it was as close as he could get.

"You're no private consultant," Scott griped as they set off.

"I'm a mailman," Will said, warming to the label. A mailman had routine in every day, and enjoyed a life beyond the job. A girlfriend or wife to take on dates. Hobbies. Family past and present to celebrate with on holidays.

He thought he could get used to that. Surprisingly, he wanted to try.

The men moved sluggishly, struggling with their injuries. Will thought it might be faster to just carry them to the trail, but squashed his impatience.

"Mailman." Scott snorted. "Right. You've cost me a major payday along with several good men."

"I didn't make you take the job," Will replied with no sympathy. "Who cares about the money? In prison I hear the currency is different."

Max groaned at that. "Damn you, Scott. I told you this sounded too good to be true."

"Is Lancaster dead?" Scott asked Will.

"Not for lack of trying to get me to kill him. Attacked me with a branch."

"Really?" Max tripped over a root and slammed into a tree. "More proof he's a lunatic. I'm not going down for a damned lunatic."

"You'll keep your mouth shut," Scott ordered.

"And let you get the better deal? No way."

"Quiet. Save it for someone who can do something with your statement," Will suggested, urging them along.

He didn't want to be away from Charly any longer than necessary. She could hold her own—and would—but he wanted this over immediately, if not sooner. He had a new life waiting for him in Durango and he wanted to get started on it. He hadn't fully appreciated the potential in this opportunity. Not until she'd opened his eyes and slipped under his well-fortified defenses.

As Charly and Lancaster came into view, Will felt himself grinning. Charly had propped Lancaster's feet up on a log, a minimal effort at first aid or comfort. Will laughed.

He tossed her the gauze and tape from the pack and kept Lancaster in line while she dressed the knife wound. "That should hold while we walk."

"I can't walk."

Will shrugged. "I'll drag you then." He

reached for Lancaster's wrists and nodded for Charly to lead on. It took less than a minute for Lancaster to change his mind.

Along the way, Scott, Max and Lancaster groused and argued, exchanging insults and threats. Will looked to Charly and in her quiet smile he found an echo of his thoughts. They both wanted to be rid of these men. He checked his watch, finally noticing it had taken a direct hit. Ah, well. It was fitting. The watch had been a tool since his first SEAL operation and those days were now behind him.

"How much farther?" he asked Charly.

She looked up to the sky, then turned a full circle. "I'd guess just over an hour at this pace."

"Good." Just over an hour until they could hand over the prisoners. A few hours of questioning, then he could get cleaned up and start moving forward with his new life.

As they ambled on, he started considering and prioritizing the best tactical approach to keep her in it with him.

CHARLY FELT THE thudding of booted feet on the ground, heard the advance well before the team rounded the curve in the trail. Relief washed over her as a black-clad tactical team, alongside men and women in local police and park ranger uniforms, surrounded them.

Lancaster's device was quickly seized by the two members from the tactical unit. The three criminals were secured with metal cuffs at wrists and ankles and linked with belly chains and marched away.

Steve, her friend from the Durango police department, approached slowly, concern etched into his face. "Are you okay?"

"Yes," she replied, leaning her hands on her knees and gulping in air. "We're fine."

"Everyone in town's been going nuts since those other two were picked up."

She gave herself a mental high five that the ploy had worked in their favor.

"Did they talk?" Will asked, stroking her back.

"Not much beyond where they were staying and who hired them," Steve said. "You'll both need to come in and answer a few questions. It can wait until tomorrow if you need some time."

Charly stood tall and linked her hand with Will's. "Let's just get it over with."

They walked down to the blacktopped parking area choked with official vehicles from various agencies. If she'd had any lingering doubts that he was working on a major government operation, this sight dispelled them.

Will raised her hand to his lips. "You go on. I'll be right behind you."

She wanted to protest, suddenly afraid to be without him for even a moment. But that was clingy and weak. She was neither. If this was the end of her time with him, she'd manage.

Somehow.

"I'll be right behind you," Will repeated, giving her hand a squeeze.

She probably shouldn't believe him. He was an undercover agent, a former SEAL, and he'd accomplished his mission. But she hoped, wished, for more time as she followed his gaze toward an oversized dark SUV with blue lights flashing from the grille and above the rearview mirror. One man, aviator sunglasses blocking his eyes, sat in the driver's seat. The tinted windows could be hiding another person or a small committee.

She stuffed her hands into her pockets as he walked away, grateful for Steve's soft-spoken explanation of what she could expect when they reached the police station in Durango.

Chapter Eighteen

His patience waning with the fading sunlight, Will waited on a bench across the street for Charly to exit the police station, heedless of the rain falling steadily as the day gave way to evening. The tidy brick building had felt small and insignificant after what they'd endured. Survived. He wanted nothing more than to take Charly home and start putting all of this behind them.

But there were details to manage when men died and his word—which should have been enough—wasn't. Evidence would be gathered. Reports filed, investigated and filed again. He reminded himself he had the utmost respect for law enforcement officials. As he felt the passing of each minute, counting them in his head, he knew it didn't take this damn long to give a statement. She shouldn't have to go through it alone, but he hadn't been allowed to join her.

He could hardly charge in there now. Lancaster was in custody, the Blackout Key had been turned over to Casey and he'd kept his promise to himself. Charly was safe.

So why weren't they done with her? He kept replaying that moment in the parking lot. He hadn't wanted to leave her, but she'd given him that look. The one that simultaneously reassured him she could manage and worried him that she didn't need him.

He made plans while he waited in the rain. He'd keep it simple, straightforward. She'd come to his apartment tonight, and he'd pour out a measure of tequila for both of them and just tell her all of it. At least the things she didn't already know.

Maybe they should stop and eat first. If they talked over dinner in a public place, he'd stay calm. The pub. That would work. He'd take her to dinner, answer any remaining questions she had for him, and then they would move forward. Together. Separately wasn't an option.

It calmed him to look at it like a mission: assess, plan and act.

Will saw Charly through the glass doors of the police station, watched her friend Steve wrap her in a gentle hug. It was nothing, Will told himself. He would comfort her from this point forward, on the rare occasions she wanted or needed comfort. Amazing and capable, that was his Charly.

The thought brought a smile to his face, and he came to his feet as she pushed the door open.

He waved, but she wasn't looking at him. Something inside caught her attention and she let the door close between them. After a short hesitation, she disappeared into the station under the arm of her cop friend.

She didn't look back.

His heart, the organ he'd thought only useful for pumping his blood, cracked. Bled. He sat down again, waiting. She would come back.

He'd believed her last night when she'd declared she wasn't done with him. If he'd misinterpreted, if she'd only meant she wasn't done with the sex, he'd count it a starting point. He'd never expected to meet a woman who wanted more than his body or money. He'd never gone looking for the kind of woman who'd encourage him to give more. But he'd damned well found her, hadn't he?

He pushed to his feet and stalked across the street, done with waiting.

"Charly left."

Will swiveled, glaring at the cop who'd spoken. "No, she didn't. I was waiting for her."

"Through the back." The cop jerked his thumb toward the back hall.

"She doesn't have her truck."

"Steve drove. She was upset."

"Naturally." Will had a plan to fix that.

A man with a singular focus, he searched the station.

"She's not here," the cop repeated when Will halted at the back door. "You should go on home."

Impossible. It was the only coherent word his mind could form. Impossible that she'd walk away without a word. He wanted to collapse. To rail. To demand an explanation. The tumultuous energy propelled him out of the station and down the street. It couldn't be over. It damn well *wasn't* over.

Will's determined stride gave way to a jog, then an all-out run as he aimed toward the Binali Backcountry store. She'd want to get her truck to go home. A slave to the emotions choking him, he ran right past her truck before he skidded to a stop. Her truck was parked on the street in front of the pub. The pub. Where he'd wanted to be anyway.

He swiped the rain from his hair and yanked open the heavy wooden door. His eyes on her, he quickly dealt with the customers who'd already heard the news of Lancaster's takedown. Shaking free of the gauntlet of congratulations, he walked straight up to where she sat perched on a stool at the end of the bar.

"What are you doing here?" he demanded roughly.

"You're wet."

"It's only water."

She turned away, asking the bartender for a towel.

His vision hazed. He couldn't take her back one more second. "Look at me." If he touched her, he'd likely toss her over his shoulder and haul her away to his apartment until they settled a few personal terms.

Barbaric, but it held a certain appeal. As plans went, sometimes improvisation was required. "You left me."

"No. I didn't. Let me explain."

"No." He crowded closer, pinning her lithe body between him and the bar.

"Will." Charly looked up into his face, feeling terrible, and terribly wanted at the same time. "I didn't leave you."

His lips, soft and hot on hers, smothered her explanation. She marveled that his clothes, rain soaked and plastered to his sculpted body, didn't just steam away from the intense heat between them. She pushed at his shoulders, for all the good it did. She might as well have been shoving at a mountain. "Will," she whispered when he eased back at last.

The hurt and confusion in his blue gaze, knowing she'd put it there, made her ache. "I didn't leave you." She got all the words out this time. "I wanted to surprise you. They said you'd gone home. I thought I'd bring a hot meal, cold beer and dessert to your place."

"Why?" His dark eyebrows slashed down into a frown she found more adorable than intimidating. He shook his head, scattering the droplets of rain clinging to his hair. "Doesn't matter. We need to talk."

"Yes." She bounced a little in her seat. She needed to tell him how she felt. Then maybe he could forgive her for what she'd just done on a wild impulse. "Yes, we do." Worried she'd overstepped, she knew she'd find a way to weather that storm if he got upset.

If? Upset was pretty much a guarantee. She stopped herself before that boulder could gather momentum.

As she'd been giving her statements, Will might as well have been in the room with her. She'd felt him that strongly. She'd given the facts, won the battle against the tears as she relived Clint's death, and managed not to do a happy dance while recounting burying her knife in Lancaster's leg.

When she thought of everything they'd overcome, she understood on a soul-deep level the motto "life is too short" that people often quoted so carelessly. She'd come down the mountain a changed woman and she'd taken the appropriate action in the aftermath.

Will needed his family—at the bare minimum he needed to give his parents a chance at reconciliation. A chance to get reacquainted with their remaining son. And she'd be there, helping him reconcile or helping him cut the ties.

Whatever life tossed at them next, they'd meet it head-on. As a team. He might not realize it yet, but she would soon make it clear he was no longer a one-man operation.

"I know that look."

"You just think you know that look." She patted the stool next to her. "The order's almost ready. Then we can go to my place and talk."

"I was going to take you to my place tonight."

She reached over and rubbed her hand across his thigh. His cargo pants were drenched, but she could feel the warmth of him under the fabric. "Maybe that is a better idea."

He could change into dry clothes and they could have a reasonable discussion before she stripped him naked and let him have his way with her. She felt her cheeks warm with anticipation.

He covered her hand with his. "So let's go. We're wasting time."

She felt the urgency nipping at her, but she needed to get the words out. "In a minute. We need food." She cleared her throat, cleared out the tension making her voice tight. "There's something I want to say first."

"I'm all ears." His thumb rubbed slow circles against her palm.

"Okay." She took a breath, considered ordering a shot to smooth out her jangling nerves. "I had Steve look up your parents." As she feared, he stopped moving, doing that turn-to-stone thing he'd done on the mountain just before he'd strike. "Hear me out," she said, chafing his hand between hers. "I want to meet your family."

"Charly."

The raw pain in his voice lanced through her heart. She barreled on. "Life's too short, Will. We can't live with regrets and questions that are too easily answered."

"Nothing's easy about my parents." He swiveled on the seat, the water from the knees of his rain-soaked pants seeping through her jeans. She felt him tremble and knew it wasn't just the cold.

"It might not be so bad," she said. "I talked to your mom."

The sound he made was some sad cross between a laugh and a snort.

"Your parents love you, I know it. They love you," she said again, "even if they were too hurt to show it the last time you talked."

"What did you tell them?"

"No revealing details, I swear. I thought about saying they'd won a trip from Binali Backcountry, but I didn't want them to blow that off. I wanted to be sure they came out. I told them you were working here, that we're friends."

He raised his eyes to hers, and that hot gaze lit up her whole system before he looked away.

"I wasn't going to tell them *that*." She cleared her throat. "Anyway. I asked them to come out and see you."

His silence unnerved her. Steve had warned her this was a mistake. He'd helped her find the right Mr. and Mrs. Chase of Illinois, but he'd warned her all the same.

Dread pooled just under her heart, threatening her resolve. She resisted the urge to backpedal. Will might not like her taking the initiative; he might not want to admit it, but he needed this. If only for closure, he needed this.

"They said yes."

"I see."

"Do you?" She dipped her head, but he was staring down at their joined hands. "Do you understand you don't have to meet them alone? I'll be with you. Right beside you." She wished like hell he'd look at her, say something. React. Good, bad or indifferent, any reaction was better than the silence. "If they're awful to you, if they don't want to try and be a family, you can tell me *I told you so* for the rest of my days. Right after I kick them to the curb."

She watched his throat work as he swallowed. Would he ever find the words to reply? She could take it, whatever he wanted to say, she told herself.

His blue eyes moved like a caress from their joined hands up and over her face. When he met her gaze, the warm tenderness made her tremble. "I love you, Charly."

"What?" She couldn't have heard him right. Of all the responses she'd expected, that wasn't it. Wasn't even in the top ten. "What did you say?" she repeated dumbly.

"You heard me." He pushed on her chin until her mouth closed. "That's why I waited for you in the rain. That's what I needed to tell you. To show you."

A delicious shiver shot down her spine. "Will."

"Right here is where I need to be. Not just for the job. Here." He tapped her knee. "Out there," he said, tilting his head toward the door. "You've changed me and I didn't even know I needed it.

You did that. Life is definitely too short to hold back the words. I love you."

She blinked away the sheen of tears blurring her vision and spied the laughter in the clear blue depths of his eyes. "Say it again."

He leaned in until they were nearly nose to nose. "Maybe later," he whispered. "After you say it back."

He meant it. The realization hit her heart with all the force of a bolt of lightning. This wasn't some ill-advised ploy to extend the connection they'd discovered on the mountain. It wasn't a tactic to keep her in his bed. Her imagination took a quick and happy detour thinking about making love with Will in the soft comfort of a real bed.

"Charly?"

She grinned at him, the happiness bubbling through her system. Of course he meant it. Will didn't say things he didn't mean. After everything they'd encountered, he sat here surrounded by half the town speaking the most powerful words she'd ever heard.

He loved her. *Her.*

"Amazing." The word slipped past her lips, an absolute truth.

He cocked his head. "That might be close enough."

"No. Not even." She hopped off the stool,

enjoyed the little wobble in her knees. She stepped in until her hips were surrounded by his strong thighs, until she could lean on the unfailing wall of his muscular chest. "I love you, too," she murmured against his lips.

She melted against him and a round of applause started, peppered with suggestions to get a room. Pulling back, peering at the onlookers, she soaked it all in. This was home, and as complete as she'd felt before Will, she felt a hundred times better now.

The bartender came out with the to-go bags, adding a bottle of champagne. "On the house for a couple of happy heroes."

"Thanks!" She reached for Will's hand, but he scooped her up into his arms. Her heart fluttered in her chest. "Seriously?"

"I'm sweeping you off your feet." He kissed her. "And I'll never break your heart."

"Same goes. You're my best fantasy come true."

"Tell me more." He winked. "I'll make them all come true. One by one."

Her pulse pounded as he swept her out of the pub to another round of cheers. She thought for sure he'd put her down once they were outside, but he carried her straight up the block to his apartment. She let her head drop to his shoulder with a happy sigh. Fantasies didn't come to life any better than her personal hero with a heart as big as the mountain.

Epilogue

Thomas Casey updated his password for his online bank access, grateful it was still possible. He didn't like thinking about the setbacks they'd be facing now if the Blackout Key hadn't been recovered.

He'd been right about Will, despite their rocky start. The new mailman in Colorado meant Thomas was one step closer to completing the task force. One step closer to retirement.

As he clicked to open the next personnel file on his computer, he hoped he could make it three for three.

* * * * *

LARGER-PRINT BOOKS!

PASSION GUARANTEED SEDUCTION

GET 2 FREE LARGER-PRINT NOVELS PLUS 2 FREE GIFTS!

YES! Please send me 2 FREE LARGER-PRINT Harlequin Presents® novels and my 2 FREE gifts (gifts are worth about $10). After receiving them, if I don't wish to receive any more books, I can return the shipping statement marked "cancel." If I don't cancel, I will receive 6 brand-new novels every month and be billed just $5.05 per book in the U.S. or $5.49 per book in Canada. That's a saving of at least 16% off the cover price! It's quite a bargain! Shipping and handling is just 50¢ per book in the U.S. and 75¢ per book in Canada.* I understand that accepting the 2 free books and gifts places me under no obligation to buy anything. I can always return a shipment and cancel at any time. Even if I never buy another book, the two free books and gifts are mine to keep forever.

176/376 HDN F43N

Name	(PLEASE PRINT)	
Address		Apt. #
City	State/Prov.	Zip/Postal Code

Signature (if under 18, a parent or guardian must sign)

Mail to the **Harlequin® Reader Service:**
IN U.S.A.: P.O. Box 1867, Buffalo, NY 14240-1867
IN CANADA: P.O. Box 609, Fort Erie, Ontario L2A 5X3

**Are you a subscriber to Harlequin Presents books
and want to receive the larger-print edition?
Call 1-800-873-8635 today or visit us at www.ReaderService.com.**

* Terms and prices subject to change without notice. Prices do not include applicable taxes. Sales tax applicable in N.Y. Canadian residents will be charged applicable taxes. Offer not valid in Quebec. This offer is limited to one order per household. Not valid for current subscribers to Harlequin Presents Larger-Print books. All orders subject to credit approval. Credit or debit balances in a customer's account(s) may be offset by any other outstanding balance owed by or to the customer. Please allow 4 to 6 weeks for delivery. Offer available while quantities last.

Your Privacy—The Harlequin® Reader Service is committed to protecting your privacy. Our Privacy Policy is available online at www.ReaderService.com or upon request from the Harlequin Reader Service.

We make a portion of our mailing list available to reputable third parties that offer products we believe may interest you. If you prefer that we not exchange your name with third parties, or if you wish to clarify or modify your communication preferences, please visit us at www.ReaderService.com/consumerschoice or write to us at Harlequin Reader Service Preference Service, P.O. Box 9062, Buffalo, NY 14269. Include your complete name and address.

HPLP13R

LARGER-PRINT BOOKS!
GET 2 FREE LARGER-PRINT NOVELS PLUS
2 FREE GIFTS!

❤ HARLEQUIN®

Romance

From the Heart, For the Heart

YES! Please send me 2 FREE LARGER-PRINT Harlequin® Romance novels and my 2 FREE gifts (gifts are worth about $10). After receiving them, if I don't wish to receive any more books, I can return the shipping statement marked "cancel." If I don't cancel, I will receive 4 brand-new novels every month and be billed just $4.84 per book in the U.S. or $5.24 per book in Canada. That's a savings of at least 19% off the cover price! It's quite a bargain! Shipping and handling is just 50¢ per book in the U.S. and 75¢ per book in Canada.* I understand that accepting the 2 free books and gifts places me under no obligation to buy anything. I can always return a shipment and cancel at any time. Even if I never buy another book, the two free books and gifts are mine to keep forever.

119/319 HDN F43Y

Name	(PLEASE PRINT)

Address	Apt. #

City	State/Prov.	Zip/Postal Code

Signature (if under 18, a parent or guardian must sign)

Mail to the **Harlequin®** Reader Service:
IN U.S.A.: P.O. Box 1867, Buffalo, NY 14240-1867
IN CANADA: P.O. Box 609, Fort Erie, Ontario L2A 5X3
Want to try two free books from another line?
Call 1-800-873-8635 or visit www.ReaderService.com.

* Terms and prices subject to change without notice. Prices do not include applicable taxes. Sales tax applicable in N.Y. Canadian residents will be charged applicable taxes. Offer not valid in Quebec. This offer is limited to one order per household. Not valid for current subscribers to Harlequin Romance Larger-Print books. All orders subject to credit approval. Credit or debit balances in a customer's account(s) may be offset by any other outstanding balance owed by or to the customer. Please allow 4 to 6 weeks for delivery. Offer available while quantities last.

Your Privacy—The Harlequin® Reader Service is committed to protecting your privacy. Our Privacy Policy is available online at www.ReaderService.com or upon request from the Harlequin Reader Service.

We make a portion of our mailing list available to reputable third parties that offer products we believe may interest you. If you prefer that we not exchange your name with third parties, or if you wish to clarify or modify your communication preferences, please visit us at www.ReaderService.com/consumerschoice or write to us at Harlequin Reader Service Preference Service, P.O. Box 9062, Buffalo, NY 14269. Include your complete name and address.

ReaderService.com

Manage your account online!

- Review your order history
- Manage your payments
- Update your address

---

*We've designed
the Harlequin® Reader Service
website just for you.*

Enjoy all the features!

- Reader excerpts from any series
- Respond to mailings and
  special monthly offers
- Discover new series available to you
- Browse the Bonus Bucks catalog
- Share your feedback

Visit us at:
ReaderService.com